TRIPLE
TROUBLE

MORE TWIN-TASTIC FUN
FROM JULIA DeVILLERS
AND JENNIFER ROY

TRIPLE TROUBLE

Julia DeVillers
Jennifer Roy

ALADDIN
NEW YORK LONDON TORONTO SYDNEY NEW DELHI

ALADDIN

An imprint of Simon & Schuster Children's Publishing Division
1230 Avenue of the Americas, New York, NY 10020
First Aladdin hardcover edition January 2013
For information about special discounts for bulk purchases, please contact Simon & Schuster Special Sales at 1-866-506-1949 or business@simonandschuster.com.
The Simon & Schuster Speakers Bureau can bring authors to your live event. For more information or to book an event contact the Simon & Schuster Speakers Bureau at 1-866-248-3049 or visit our website at www.simonspeakers.com.
Designed by Karin Paprocki
The text of this book was set in Granjon.
Manufactured in the United States of America 1112 FFG
2 4 6 8 10 9 7 5 3 1
Library of Congress Cataloging-in-Publication Data
DeVillers, Julia.
Triple trouble / Julia DeVillers, Jennifer Roy. — 1st Aladdin hardcover ed.
p. cm.
Summary: While continuing to switch places in middle school, identical twins Payton and Emma compete with triplets Dexter, Oliver, and Asher at the Multipalooza festival.
ISBN 978-1-4424-3405-9
[1. Twins—Fiction. 2. Sisters—Fiction. 3. Impersonation—Fiction. 4. Competition (Psychology)—Fiction. 5. Triplets—Fiction. 6. Middle schools—Fiction. 7. Schools—Fiction.]
I. Roy, Jennifer Rozines, 1967– II. Title.
PZ7.D4974Ts 2013
[Fic]—dc23
2012019624
ISBN 978-1-4424-3407-3 (eBook)

To our agents,
Mel Berger (WME) and
Alyssa Eisner Henkin (TMG)

Payton

One

FIRST PERIOD, STUDY HALL

autumn dance!
TICKETS ON SALE NOW!

I stared at the poster hanging on the wall in the hallway near my homeroom. My first middle school dance! So exciting! So scary! Exciting! Scary! *Yay! Eek! Yay!*

I was excited because I mean, Yay! My very first dance! So yay! But also eek!

The eek part was that it was our first school dance *and* I was going with a date. Yes, Nick had asked me to the dance! My first dance! My first date! My mom said okay since we were going all together in a group with our other friends. But Nick would be my date.

My first dance! My first date! What would we talk about? Could Nick dance? Would we slow dance? What if we slow danced and my hands got sweaty?

"Miss Mills," a voice called out, "will you be joining us?"

It was my homeroom teacher, Mrs. "Bad Breath" Galbreath.

Bad breath. I hadn't even thought of that. Oh no! What if I was slow dancing with Nick and I had bad breath? What if—

I snapped out of it. I guess I should be focusing on *What if Mrs. Galbreath gives me detention for being late?* I had an iffy history of getting in trouble in middle school, so I raced to the classroom.

"Sorry!" I said weakly as I slid under Mrs. Galbreath's arm while she was shutting the door.

Whew! Made it.

I slid into a seat near the back and set my tote bag down on the floor next to me. I scrounged around for my social studies homework. I felt my brush and mini-mirror. My papaya-flavored lip gloss (that I'd bought in Hollywood). Sunglasses (that I'd worn in Hollywood—I didn't need them here). I really needed to clean out my tote bag.

And there it was: my social studies binder. I pulled it out and put it on my desk.

I'd promised my parents that missing school for HOLLYWOOD wouldn't interfere with my school-work. Sigh. Hollywood was over. No more starring in commercials, being on TV game shows, taking glamorous convertible rides, or bumping into celebrities and having my name linked to them. No more being famous. But lots more social studies.

And if I didn't keep my grades up, there would be "consequences." My parents had already once "limited my after-school activities" because of my grades. They just started letting me participate in drama club *and* VOGS (our middle school's video broadcast show) again. If I didn't get my schoolwork caught up, they might take those away again.

Or the punishment could be worse! What if they grounded me? Oh no! They wouldn't ground me from the *dance*, would they?

Don't panic, Payton, I told myself. I would focus on my schoolwork and let nothing distract me. Question one: What are the three export products of the country of . . .

I struggled to remember the answer from the chapter I'd read last night. There were times I wished I had Emma's brain. My twin sister, Emma, could read a textbook and remember practically all the answers not just the next day, but for the rest of her life. Emma would have no problem making up her schoolwork from the days we missed.

Emma would never get grounded because of her grades. *She* would never get grounded from her very first middle school dance.

Oh yes! Emma was going to the dance too! Emma had a date too. Ox had asked her to the dance. He'd asked me yesterday what color Emma's dress was so he could get her a matching corsage. Emma's dress was so pretty. Her fashion had definitely improved this year. She'd picked out a white dress that had purple flowers all over it. My dress was a jewel-toned sapphire blue. Even though blue was Emma's signature color, I'd seen it and knew one of us would have to wear it. Emma didn't like it, so it became mine, mine, mine.

Okay, enough thinking about the dance. No more distractions, Payton. What are the three export products of the country of . . .

The door to Study Hall opened, and a guy I'd never

seen before walked in. He had straight black hair that flopped a little over his face. He was wearing an olive-colored shirt, skinny jeans, and skater shoes.

I wasn't the only one distracted. Everyone turned to look at him.

"You must be our new student," Mrs. Galbreath said. "Welcome. Take any empty seat."

The guy didn't seem bothered when everyone looked at him. He walked my way and sat down in the empty seat right behind me.

"Please return to your studies, students," Mrs. Galbreath said so everyone would stop checking out the new guy. I returned my attention to my homework. Okay. Three export products of . . .

"Psst." The new guy tapped my shoulder.

I turned around.

"It *is* you," he said. "I thought so."

Oh! I'd been recognized. He must have seen our TV commercial and knew who I was. I felt so famous!

"Hi," I whispered, smiling a nice, friendly smile so he'd know I wasn't a stuck-up celebrity and I hadn't let fame go to my head. Then I stopped smiling when I saw Galbreath looking at me. I turned back around.

Three export products of . . .

Poke, poke. The guy was poking my back again.

"Hey," the guy whispered. "Can you do me a favor?"

He slid a piece of paper toward me.

Oh! Oooh! He must want my autograph! Blush. You can take the girl out of Hollywood, but you can't take the Hollywood out of the girl! Hee hee.

I took the paper from him and wrote my signature across the back of the paper:

Payton Mills ☆

I reached over and dropped the paper back on his desk. Then I turned around and faced my social studies homework. Such was the life of a tween star. Trying to balance Hollywood and homework.

"Psst." The new guy tapped my shoulder again. Yeesh, how do Hollywood celebrities ever get their homework done? I checked to see if Galbreath was watching us. She was, but she nodded at me to help the new guy. I turned around.

"You didn't do it," he whispered.

Confused, I pointed to my signature. I was even more confused when the guy flipped over the paper to the other side.

"No, I need you to do the math problems." He lowered his voice and looked around. "See? I'm new, and I have to take some placement test to see what math class I'll be in."

What?

"Someone said you were a math genius," he whispered. "So, can you just write the answers in there? You can miss a couple to make it more authentic."

Ohhh. He thought I was my twin sister. And he thought I—meaning Emma—would help him cheat. Um, no.

"Sorry, I'm not a math genius," I whispered back. "That's my twin. She's the math genius in the family."

"Oh, you've got one of those too?" He nodded. "So do I. But wait, are you any good at math at all? Can you just do this anyway? I hate math."

"Um, isn't a placement test supposed to help you get into the right math class?" I asked.

"Whatever," he said. "I have family pressure to get in advanced classes."

"Well, if it makes you feel any better, I know the feeling," I said. "Although my family is used to it. My sister is four grades ahead of me in math. And we're even identical twins! That's why you mixed us up."

Yes, sometimes even I almost mixed us up. Like one time in a clothes store I went over and started talking to her. But then I realized it was a full-length mirror.

But there are differences!

I'm PAYTON, the twin who
- is one inch taller.
- has slightly greener eyes.
- definitely, without a doubt, has shinier hair—today, at least.

Today Emma definitely was not shiny, shiny, double the shiny. This morning she'd put her unwashed hair in a scrunchie. A green scrunchie! Fortunately, I'd had an extra rubber band in my tote bag and convinced her to change it. Otherwise, she would have embarrassed us. Yes, us. When you're an identical twin, there's always the chance that people will think your twin is you.

And I didn't want anyone thinking I'd wear a green scrunchie. Emma had to represent the Mills Twins better.

Sometimes being a twin could be annoying. Being *Emma's twin* could be seriously annoying. Like sibling rivalry times two. She's been cranky. And not very well dressed. I know she's been feeling stressed, but we were just in a shampoo commercial, representing good hair, yet she had put her hair up in a scrunchie?

Like I told her before homeroom: Represent the Mills Twins, Emma. Represent.

Two

EARLIER . . . BEFORE HOMEROOM

I had just shrugged off my jacket and hung it up in my locker when my twin sister made a sound like *"Agh!"*

"Agh?" I said. "What's agh?"

"Emma," Payton said, ignoring my question. "Why do you look like that?"

"Like what?" I responded irritably. I looked at myself in my locker mirror. Oh. My grumpy face. "I look this way because of Jazmine James! She got my science fair project disqualified from the competition, remember?"

"Of course I remember," my twin said. "You haven't shut up about it."

"She accused me of unethical research!" I complained. "Which is impossible since I hadn't *begun* the research; I was still in the proposal stage and seeing if lip reading was even a viable topic. But now it's too late to enter!"

"Emma—" Payton hissed.

"It's unacceptable" I ranted. "There's a competition going on, and I'M NOT IN IT!"

"Emma, quiet down." Payton shut her locker door. "Now you're embarrassing me for TWO reasons. Yes, it stinks you're not in the science fair, but you WON the whole Mathletes competition down in New York City."

"That was so last month," I said, dismissing her. "You're only as great as your last win. And last week, Jazmine James won the school Geobee."

"Only because we were in Hollywood," Payton said. "Remember?"

Yeah. Okay. That was a lot of fun. But middle school was not supposed to be fun and games. I was losing my edge; couldn't Payton see the problem?

"The problem," Payton said, "is why do you look like that? Like the old Emma, the first-day-of-middle-school Emma who wore schlumpy clothes and didn't care at all about how she looked? And also didn't care that people might confuse her with her identical twin sister and think YOU are ME?"

I grabbed my books and closed my locker. Then I looked down at what I was wearing. OH. I'd thrown on my clothes in the dark this morning and apparently hadn't noticed that my brown oversized hoodie clashed with my black track pants. And holey orange sneakers.

Payton was kind of right. But I was in no mood to let her know.

"Payton, I have more important things to think about," I told her.

"And your hair," Payton continued. "I thought you took pride in being the twin with the shinier hair. Not that it's true, of course. Mine is shinier. But today your hair is totally shineless."

"Hmmm," I mumbled. "I guess I forgot to wash it." I pulled a green scrunchie out of my hoodie pocket and quickly put my hair up.

"There." I looked at my sister. "It's fixed."

"Emma!" Payton shrieked. "We have a year's supply of Teen Sheen shampoo! We are their national spokest-wins!"

"Now who's being embarrassing?" I said. "Shh! I'm

sorry your priorities are superficial and shallow, but I don't have time for this. I'm going to homeroom."

"Not with that scrunchie you're not," Payton said. She reached out and ripped it out of my hair. "Don't move."

"Ow!" I rubbed my head as she scrounged around in her tote bag. She handed me a regular ponytail band, and after I threw my hair up, I stomped away without saying bye.

"Represent the Mills Twins, Emma," Payton called after me. "Represent!"

I felt a little bad, stomping away without saying bye, but sometimes being a twin was irritating. Being Payton's twin was seriously irritating. Like sibling rivalry times two. Still. I had been a little too harsh. I'd catch up with her later and explain how stressed I was.

"Hi, Emma!" I looked down the hallway. There was my friend Quinn. She was standing outside my homeroom with . . . Ox.

Ox, my more-than-a-friend-but-less-than-a-boyfriend.

"Ox is helping me put up my posters," Quinn said as I got closer. "I needed someone tall to help me."

"Cute poster," I told her. *And cute boy hanging up that*

poster . . . Ox. With his brown hair and his hazel eyes, which were now looking at me.

"Done," Ox said. "Hey, Emma. Quinn, you're a really good artist."

"Thanks," Quinn smiled. "I know dancing geckos are pretty weird, but my art teacher told me I had to use our school mascot."

"No, it's great," I said. It was true—I liked her artwork. What I DIDN'T like so much were the words on it: autumn dance! tickets on sale now!

Ulp.

"The dance is going to be so much fun," Quinn said excitedly. Her brown ponytail bounced as if it were excited too. "I'm so happy you guys will both be there."

Yep. We would. Me and Ox. Like a date. A couple. Where we would have to . . . dance. I started feeling dizzy. I did not dance. I had no idea how to dance. The thought of Ox and me on a dance floor made me start to hyperventilate. I was going to make a fool of myself! In front of Ox—and the whole school.

"Uh," I said weakly. "I've got to get to homeroom." I turned and crashed right into someone.

OOF!

"Watch where you're going!" a familiar voice hissed.

"Jazmine Jones," I said through gritted teeth. I stepped back and faced my arch nemesis. *Groan.* Jazmine looked as stylish as ever, with her dark braids in perfect rows and her designer outfit with platform heels.

"Oh, hi, Emma," Jazmine said in a sticky-sweet voice. "I'll see you in science class. I'm handing in my final draft for the science fair. How about you . . . oh, I forgot. You're not going to be in it."

"Too bad, so sad," Hector cackled. Hector was Jazmine's omnipresent sidekick.

"Oh, by the way, Emma," Quinn said, jumping into the conversation. "I cannot wait to see your new dress for the dance!"

"You," Jazmine said, her eyes raised, "are going to a school dance? Aren't you afraid to fall behind?"

"Or fall on your face," snickered Hector.

I froze. Because I knew the answer.

YES. To both. I'm afraid I'll fall behind in my schoolwork and studying if I keep taking weekends off to do so-called fun activities. And, of course, I am terrified of wiping out on the dance floor.

"Hey, Hector." Ox swooped in behind me. "And Jazzie."

"It's Jazmine," Jazmine said through gritted teeth.

I relaxed a little. Ox knew what these two were like.

"Has Emma told you yet about her new project?"

"My wha—?" I started to say, but Ox nudged me. He leaned down and whispered, "Just go with it."

"Oh . . . right! That project," I sputtered. "Well, it's still sort of a secret."

Jazmine's eyes narrowed.

Ha. Keep her guessing.

"Anyway, time for homeroom," I said cheerily. "Bye, Quinn! Bye, Ox!" I waved and turned and for the second time that morning. . . .

I crashed into something.

BAM!

OW!

I'd walked smack into the CLOSED homeroom door.

It was like slow motion:

First, I crashed into the door.

Then I flew backward into the air . . .

Lost hold of backpack on way down . . .

To the floor . . .

Whoomp! I landed flat in the middle of the hallway. I shut my eyes to regroup a little bit. And to avoid seeing the crowd of people stepping around me.

"Emma!" I heard Ox's voice. "Are you okay?"

I groaned. This was superembarrassing.

"I think she hit her head!" Quinn's voice said.

My head? Oh no! I hoped my brain was working. I quickly ran through the first ten digits of pi. Easy. Whew.

"Emma, open your eyes," Ox said worriedly.

I sighed. I couldn't avoid the humiliation forever. I opened my eyes and began to get up.

"I'm all right," I said, grabbing on to the hand Ox was holding out.

"I've got Emma's backpack," Quinn said. "We should take her to the nurse's office."

"No nurse!" I said. "No, really, I'm fine." I smiled at Quinn to reassure her. Ox pulled me up, and I stood confidently upright.

"See?" I announced loudly so that the people left in the hall would hear. Like Jazmine and Hector, who were snickering nearby. "I'm fine! So I'll just head into homeroom—"

Uh.

Standing a little farther down the hall was a boy I'd never seen before. He had black hair and was wearing an olive-colored shirt, and he was staring at me.

And then he multiplied into two.

Double vision! I was experiencing double vision!

I squeezed my eyes closed and opened them again.

Oh no! It was worse! Now there were three! Three of the exact same person!

Triple vision!!!

Maybe the fall DID damage my brain! I shut my eyes again. Triple vision??? I suddenly felt very, very dizzy.

"Or," I said meekly, "I could go to the nurse after all."

Three

IN HOMEROOM

Psst. It was the new guy. Again.

Now what? Homeroom was almost over, and I hadn't finished my homework, which was due first period. At least it was in this same classroom. I'd have a few more minutes while everyone changed classes.

"I've got this teacher for social studies next," the boy whispered. "Is she easy?"

Great. He was in my social studies class. Just great. Would he try to cheat off me in that class too?

"No," I whispered back. "And I'm not my sister, so don't ask me for 'help' in there either."

"So, do you have a headache too?" he asked.

"What?" I answered. "Why would I have a headache?"

"You know, that twin question? If one twin gets hurt, does the other feel it? I guess in your case, the answer is no," he said.

"What are you talking about?"

"Didn't anyone tell you? Your twin hit her head a little while ago. BAM! Total wipeout. They took her to the nurse."

Oh no! Suddenly it didn't matter that Emma's hair wasn't shiny or that she wore a scrunchie on her head. Emma was hurt! All that mattered was that she was okay!

I waved my hand in the air to get permission to leave class.

"Sorry, I didn't know you didn't know," the new guy said. "Hope it didn't screw up her genius brain."

Emma! Her brain! I jumped up and ran out of the classroom.

Emma

Four

NURSE'S OFFICE

"Are you sure you feel okay?" The school nurse bent over me and peered at me.

I looked at the nurse. Yes, one nurse. The simple, elegant number of one, not two blurry nurses or three blurry nurses. That was an enormous relief.

"I feel fine," I said. "But perhaps you could check to see if my pupils are dilated, just in case."

I held up the little flashlight/pen/key chain I'd gotten at last year's state spelling bee and switched it on.

Bzzzt!

"What was that?" The nurse jumped back.

"My flashlight/pen/key chain that I got at a spelling

bee." I showed her. "It buzzes like a bee. A bee, for a spelling bee—get it?"

Suddenly there was a louder *buzz* from a different direction.

"That's my phone," the nurse said rushing away from my cot. "Stay right there, honey."

"Honey?" I called after her. "Like from a beehive?" Heh. Bee puns.

I flicked my flashlight off and on a few times while the nurse talked on the phone. *Bzzzt. Bzzzt.* I clipped the key chain back on my backpack and fidgeted around on the cot where I'd been stuck for the last twenty-one minutes. Twenty-one minutes gone meant there was only twenty-five minutes left of science class. Subtracting the three and a half minutes it would take me to walk to class, that would only leave twenty two and a half minutes left of science.

I couldn't miss an entire science class and let Jazmine get ahead of me. I also had to turn in my plan for the science fair today, so I had to get my A game ready. *A* for *AcadEmma*.

"Excuse me," I told the nurse, trying to sound as stable and rational as possible. "I'm one hundred percent fine. Here, I'll prove it. Ask me to spell any word in the dictionary. Or do a math problem. Precalc. Calculus. Multivariable."

"That won't be necessary," the nurse said. "Your vitals are fine, and there's no evidence of a concussion. I told your father on the phone just now I think you *are* fine. You can go back to class as soon as I write you a pass."

Excellent! I hopped up. AcadEmma was ready! She didn't let a little thing like a bump on the head get in the way of her academic focus, especially when a Jazmine James takeover was looming on the horizon! That's right! AcadEmma let nothing get her way! Noth—

"Look out!" Two boys raced into the nurse's office. Well, one raced in yelling and the other stumbled in, groaning. Then the other one threw up, right by the nurse's desk.

"We have a puker," the nurse announced. "Emma, lie back down and I'll write your pass after I take care of the vomiter."

"If you write it fast, I could get back to class and—" I hadn't finished the sentence before the kid went "Blaaaaagh" and vomited large chunks on the floor. The nurse raced off to him.

Sigh. AcadEmma was on hold. I stayed on the cot. This might take a few minutes. I closed my eyes and began silently reciting the classification of zoological species for fun.

"Blaaaagh."

Oof! Someone had knocked me back onto the cot. And was hugging me wildly.

"Glarg!" I attempted to speak, but my twin had her arms wrapped tightly around my esophagus.

"The nurse said you're okay! You're okay! I was freaking out!" Payton said dramatically.

I would have told her I was fine, but she was hugging my larynx.

"I was so worried!" Payton continued. "At first I thought, What if Emma gets amnesia and forgets that she even has a twin? I'm so happy you didn't forget me! And then I thought, Wait, what if Emma has a brain injury?"

Payton gasped. "If you broke your brain, that would change everything, Emma," Payton babbled on. "Suddenly I'd be the smart twin!"

"Sorry to disappoint," I said, twisting so she was no longer cutting off my speech. "No brain injury. Except maybe from you just now cutting off my oxygen."

"Oh!" Payton loosened her grip. "Sorry. I'm just so relieved you're okay."

It was nice of my sister to care about me so much. Even though we were so different, we were this close when it came to important things.

"I am okay," I said loudly, for the nurse's benefit. Then I lowered my voice. ". . . now. But right after I hit my head, I started seeing triple.

"Whoa. But you're really okay?" Payton said. She held up three fingers. "How many fingers am I holding up?"

"Three," I said.

"No, just one." Payton frowned. "Oh no! You're still seeing triple!"

Wait, wha—?!

"Kidding!" Payton laughed. "LOL."

"Don't mess with my brain," I scolded her.

"Hey." Payton wrinkled her nose. "What stinks?"

"A puker," I said motioning toward the front area of the nurse's office. "The nurse is going to write me a pass to leave as soon as she takes care of him. Which I hope is soon because I need to get to science class. I'm missing it now. Bad timing."

"It was good timing for me," Payton said. "I can always use a break from homework. Oh, that reminds me. There's a new guy in my class. He was the one who told me you fell. He said he saw you. Did you see him?"

"Yeah," I said. "I saw him all right." Three times, I saw him.

"He thought I was you," Payton said. "He's been here about five minutes, and he mixed us up already. He asked me to help him with his math because he heard I was a math genius."

I smiled. My reputation as a genius was known to even the newest of students.

Well, that was a plus. At least his impression of me wasn't just me hitting my head and lying on the floor.

"Did you tell him that we're twins?" I asked her.

"Yeah," Payton said, but then frowned. "He actually didn't ask me for help. He wanted me—*you*—to cheat."

"Cheat on math?" I asked.

"He had that math assessment thing to figure out what math class he's going to be in," Payton said. "He asked me to do it for him."

I've always had my share of people who try to copy my homework, sneak looks at my test paper, or pass me at my locker with a casual "Hey, Emma! What's three x minus fourteen times pi?" knowing I'd answer their homework question accidentally without thinking twice.

I was used to it. Payton looked really bothered by it, though.

"Maybe you were confused," I said. "He *is* new. But if he asks again, feel free to use my standard response: 'Nullum! Cheaters nunquam prosperabitur.'"

"What?" Payton said.

"That 'No! Cheaters never prosper,'" I told her. "In Latin. I find if you say it in Latin, it's very effective. People are confused so they don't know how to respond. Or they think it's a wizard spell I'm putting on them, and that scares them off."

Payton looked at me, shaking her head.

"What? It's effective." I shrugged.

"Your brain is so weird," Payton said. "But I'm so glad it's working."

"It's nice to see twins so caring of each other." The nurse's voice startled both of us.

We smiled at her.

"And," the nurse continued, arching her eyebrow, "it's also nice to see you together at all and not pretending to be each other by hiding out sick in the nurse's office."

Oops. When we switched places the first time, Payton had pretended to be sick so I could go to class as her. She'd slept the afternoon away on this very cot.

"I have to admit, I am fascinated by twins," the nurse said. "I didn't mean to overhear, but were you speaking in your secret twin language?"

Payton and I looked confused.

"When you said something like 'Nullum something something?'" the nurse explained.

"Actually no, I was just speaking Latin," I explained to her.

"Oh." The nurse looked disappointed, then brightened. "Well, still, you don't always hear twins speaking Latin to each other either! Let me give you both passes back to class."

The nurse handed us passes, and we headed out the door.

"Well, back to the grind," Payton said as we walked down the hall. "Hey, what are three export products of Brazil?"

"Sugar," I said automatically. "And—wait, I'm not doing your social studies work for you."

"Almost had you," Payton said, and grinned.

"Mills Twins!" One of the school secretaries came up the hallway toward us. "I heard you were both here. I have notes for each of you from the office."

She handed one envelope to Emma and one to me. We thanked her as she walked away.

"I wonder what it is," Payton said as she started to open hers. "I hope we're not in trouble!"

"You will be in trouble if you don't have a hall pass."

We turned around to see Ox's cousin and drama club member Sam behind us. Sam was wearing a hall monitor badge.

"*You're* a hall monitor?" Payton asked him.

"Correct," he said. "May I see your pass, please?"

We held out our passes.

"Hmmm." He inspected them. "They look valid. Go ahead to your classes."

"In a minute," Payton said, holding up her half-open envelope. "We just have to look at these—"

"No loitering," Sam said, shaking his head. "No dawdling or lollygagging. Move along. You need to go to your classes."

I didn't need twin telepathy to decipher Payton's eye roll. But Sam was right. I needed to get to science ASAP and show Jazmine and the world that my brain was unharmed.

For the remaining eleven minutes of class, I would think about nothing else but world domination of science. World DomEmmation.

Payton

Five

BACK TO CLASS

I opened the envelope and read the note as I walked down the hall to class.

> *From the Desk of Principal Patel*
> *Dear Ms. Mills:*
> *We are pleased to request your presence in the principal's office immediately after first period this morning.*

Oh no, I had to go to the principal's office? Was I in trouble? Wait, Emma had gotten a note too. Were we in trouble? Oh no. Oh no! What could we be in trouble for? It couldn't be a Twin Switch.

No, wait. It said "pleased to request your presence." The principal wouldn't write that if I was in trouble, right? Or did it make principals pleased to get students in trouble? I started rereading the note as I continued walking around a corner. Dear Ms. Mills—

OOF!

I walked right into someone.

"Sorry!" I said. Oh, it was the new guy. He dropped some papers he was carrying.

"Watch where you're going," he mumbled.

"Um, yeesh, sorry. It was an accident," I said as I stooped down to pick up a piece of paper he had dropped. It was a bright yellow hall pass, like mine.

"Getting out of study hall?" I asked him.

"No, orchestra," he said. He took the pass and kept on walking.

Yeesh and yeesh. I guess he was mad at me for not helping him cheat on the math thing. Well, that's his problem. He said he was going to orchestra, so maybe he got switched out of my study hall. That might not be a bad thing. I was still a little annoyed at how he had just treated me. I mean, he was new and all, so maybe he was a little overwhelmed, but still.

I reached for the door to the study hall classroom,

but it opened just as I reached for it. Someone was coming out.

"Oh, hey," I said.

Wait a minute. Did I just bump into the new guy . . . again?

I turned around, but the hallway was definitely empty now. Huh. I shook my head. That was weird. The guy was in the hall around the corner, and then he was in the hall outside. How did he move so fast?

Seriously weird. Oh, well, anyway. I had other things to think about. Like catching up on the social studies I'd missed. Eep, I'd wasted most of class in the nurse's office, and I only knew one of the three export products of the country of Brazil. I sighed and went into class. Where the guy was still sitting in his seat. Not roaming the halls.

I saw someone walk by the classroom door, and hey, there was the new guy walking by. Then he doubled.

Yes, there he was. Twice. Black hair, olive-colored shirt, skinny jeans. Times two. I shook my head to clear it.

"Psst." I tapped the girl in front of me on the shoulder. "Did you just see anyone walk by the door?" I asked her after she turned around.

"No," she said.

The girl spun back around and faced forward.

I kept looking out the door. The guy had definitely multiplied. I thought about Emma saying she had triple vision. Maybe that twin thing *was* happening: When one of you gets hurt, does the other one feel it? Maybe since Emma had hit her head and had triple vision, I was experiencing triple vision too!

I had always thought that was a stupid twin question. But could it be true? I pinched my arm and wondered if Emma could feel it. Ouch. I now had a red mark on my arm, and since we weren't allowed to use cell phones in school, there was no way to test the results.

The final minutes of class ticked by. I did as much of my social studies as I could without my textbook. I watched the clock tick. I brushed my hair. I put on some lip gloss (vanilla cupcake–scented). Then class was over, and I headed to the principal's office.

On the way, I saw Tess in the hallway. She was easy to spot because she was taller than almost everyone and I could see her blond French braid. I hurried to catch up with her.

"Hi, Payton!" Tess said. "What's up?"

I could trust Tess. Maybe she knew what was going on.

"I have to go to the principal's office," I said in a low voice. "I don't know why, though."

"Oh, I hope everything's okay," Tess said. "Maybe it's about Emma hitting her head and they're just following up."

"Maybe," I said. "Except the letter said 'We are pleased to request your presence.' They wouldn't be pleased about Emma hitting her head, I hope."

"Pleased?" Tess said. "Oh, then that's great! It's something positive. Hey, I bet I know what it is. Have they congratulated you on your commercial in Hollywood?"

Hmmm. No.

"I bet that's it!" Tess said. "They'll thank you and Emma for representing our school."

"That makes total sense." I brightened up. "Cool. Thanks, Tess."

"See you in drama!" Tess said.

I felt much better as I headed down the stairs and to the principal's office.

"Right on time," the school secretary said. "And congratulations to you! You must feel so proud."

"Thanks!" Well, it was looking like Tess was right. Whew! I wasn't in trouble. This was great!

"You can leave your bag here and go right on into the principal's office conference room," the secretary said. "Do you know where that is?"

"Yes." I sighed. It was where Emma and I had our meeting with the principal and our parents and teachers after Twin Switch Fail Number One, the first week of school. At least now the room would bring better memories! I went down the short hallway and saw that the door was slightly open.

"And here she is!" Principal Patel said. "Our star!"

Yay! That's me!

I smiled my best "commercial" smile at the small group of people sitting in chairs. They looked very official, in suits and dresses and other businessy things. A few of them smiled back. A few did not.

Eeps.

"Hello," I said. I felt a little awkward standing there while they all looked at me, but hey, I wanted to be an actress, so I would pretend this was an audition.

"This is our esteemed school board as well as a few members of the state department of educational success," the principal said. "You may recognize them."

I went along with it and nodded. Principal wanted to show off? Okay! I'd redeem myself for all my past wrongs. Now, where was Emma?

"We're very proud," one of the women said.

"Thank you," I said, smiling. How nice. I shook

out my hair a little so they could see the shiny hair and friendly "everygirl" look that had won us the role. (That's what the Hollywood director had told us.)

"Would you mind demonstrating some of your prowess to us, Ms. Mills?" one of the women asked me.

"Sure?" I hesitated. Okay, I wasn't sure what *prowess* was. Why wasn't Emma here yet? She would know what the word meant and how to respond. I'd have to wing it without her. I took a guess that it meant I was supposed to show off our lines.

"I love having shiny hair. Shiny hair makes me feel shiny inside," I said brightly.

I swished my hair, just the way the director had told me they liked. Swish! Swish!

The audience stopped smiling. Hmmm. Swish! I swished harder. The audience looked confused, annoyed, and amused. But not impressed. Okay, I'd try again.

"Um. Teen Sheen shampoo? That's what makes your hair so supershiny?" I continued. Still the same response. Not smiling. Well, I'd saved the best for last. I saw one of the people had a water bottle on the table, and I reached over and grabbed it.

I held it up to my face as if it were a bottle of Teen Sheen shampoo and smiled my best dazzling smile.

"'Shiny, shiny, double the shiny!'" I said. Yes! I had nailed that line, if I did say so myself. However, my audience was not applauding, or asking for my autograph. Actually, they looked a little freaked out. Two of them murmured to each other.

"Ah, heh-heh." the principal gave a nervous laugh. "Ms. Mills is demonstrating her *other* talent: acting. Yes, she and her twin sister were recently featured on a national television commercial."

Everyone in the room went "Ohhh!" and started nodding like they got it. But I didn't get it.

Principal continued. "Does anyone have a question?"

Yes, actually, me! I had a question. If they weren't talking about the commercial, why was I here? What questions were they going to ask me? And where the heck was Emma?!?!

"Ahem." One of the men cleared his throat. "What was your winning question and answer?"

"Winning question in . . . ?" I asked nervously.

"Oh!" Principal said. "I need to be more clear. She's so brilliant, she wins many competitions—science, Geobee, spelling. We're talking about your recent win in Mathletes. What was the winning question and answer?"

Oh. OH! Oh. Uh-oh.

They thought I was Emma! You could probably see the lightbulb go off over my head right then. I must have accidentally gotten a letter for my sister.

"I'm not—" I started to explain, but Principal Patel looked kind of desperate. I realized she had brought me/Emma in to show off. I didn't want to embarrass her. Okay, I just had to answer one question and—ta-da!—all would be fine.

The good news was, I knew the answer to that question! Yes, I did! Not that I would have been able to figure out the math problem myself, obviously. But because after the competition, Emma kept saying it in the car on the way home.

"They asked me that angle blah blah secant problem!" She kept saying over and over, endlessly. "And I answered forty percent! And then they said, 'That is correct! Emma Mills is the Mathletes champion!'"

Her reliving that moment had drilled it into my skull. Phew. Right now I was thankful that my sister had been so totally annoying! I repeated what Emma said.

Everyone at the table murmured approvingly and applauded me. Awesome! I did a little bow, like I thought Emma would do.

This was working out just fine. Actually, it was a

good thing they had mistakenly called me in because Emma was so stressed and well, messy, today. In her sweats and with her unwashed look, she wasn't really representing.

"Emma, to what do you owe your math success?" somebody asked.

I caught Principal Patel's eye. Okay, Payton. Think like Emma.

"Well, I have great advanced-math teachers, and I'm able to take advanced courses online too," I said. Everyone nodded, so I went on, encouraged. "And of course, I couldn't do it with my fabulous twin sister, Payton!"

"Ah, two skilled mathematicians in one family?" a woman said.

Wait, uh, no. Let's not go there.

"Well!" I said brightly. "I should probably get to my . . ." Second period . . . Emma had . . . um . . . some class.

"Oh, I'll write you an excuse," Principal Patel said. "We have time for a few more questions."

"Ms. Mills, what is an asymptote?" the woman asked me.

Um. Uh. Er. I broke out into a sweat so cold I probably looked as unwashed as Emma. Um. Uh. What should I do? I didn't want to embarrass the principal. So I did the first thing that came to mind.

I sneezed. I did the biggest, grossest fake sneeze that I could possibly fake.

"Excuse me!" I gasped. "The answer is . . . achoo!"

I held my arm up to my mouth and sneezed harder. Then I went into a cough-choking-gag noise.

"Emma! Are you okay?" the principal asked.

"Water!" I gasped, and pointed to the hallway.

"Goodness, well, perhaps you should go to the water fountain," one of the woman said authoritatively. "Thank you for sharing your accomplishments with us, Emma."

I backed out of the room and fled down the hall before they could stop me. I didn't stop until I had fast-walked up the stairs and into the empty hallway. I leaned against a locker to catch my breath.

Whew. Emma might have academic awards, but I deserved an *Academy Award* for that performance!

Emma

Six

ALSO BACK TO CLASS

I slid the note into my tote bag as I walked quickly to my science class. The note I'd gotten from the principal's office. All it said was:

Please report to Classroom B13 at 10:43.
Mrs. Burkle

I assumed Payton had gotten the same note. Last time we'd had a special meeting with Mrs. Burkle, we'd ended up going off to Hollywood. I didn't know what to expect this time, but I hoped it didn't add to my workload. I couldn't worry about it now. Right now I needed to focus, and my focus was 100 percent science. I pushed open the door to my science class. Everyone looked at me as I walked in.

". . . are called metamorphic rocks." Dr. Perkins stopped her lecture and looked at me. "Emma, I'll take your pass, and you may have a seat."

I handed her my pass and tried to head unobtrusively to my usual seat in the second row. Except someone was in it. Someone had stolen my prime seat. I scanned the room, ignoring Jazmine's smirk. The only empty seat was in the back, behind Cashmere.

I hated sitting in the back. Plus Cashmere had really big hair that was hard to see over. But I sat down and listened to Dr. Perkins.

"What are metamorphic rocks with mineral crystals arranged in parallel layers called?" Dr. Perkins asked.

My science teacher hadn't even finished the question before my hand shot up. Jazmine James raised her hand at least three milliseconds after mine, but since she was sitting in the prime seat in front-row center, the teacher must have seen her first.

"Jazmine?"

"Foliated," Jazmine answered.

Whatever. That was an easy question. I'd save myself for a more challenging question.

"Class, what is an example of a mpppf mpppf rock?"

What? What had she said? Dr. Perkins had turned toward the chalkboard, so I couldn't hear the end of the question. I tapped Cashmere in front of me. Her hair wasn't blocking as much as usual because she was leaning forward, as if she were trying hard to hear as well.

"Psst, Cashmere," I whispered. "What did the teacher say?"

"Yes!" Cashmere's head suddenly jerked up, and she shouted, "Yes, I'll marry you, Ron Weasley!"

Half the class—including me—jumped. And then everyone except me started cracking up.

"Wha—? Where am I?" Cashmere sputtered.

"I'm sorry, did I wake you up?" Dr. Perkins said sarcastically.

"No," Cashmere said. "You didn't. Emma did. She jabbed me in the back."

Everyone turned to look at me. Ahem.

"Jabbing is frowned upon." Dr. Perkins frowned at me.

"Sorry," I mumbled.

"But sleeping in class is also frowned upon, Cashmere," Dr. Perkins said. "Although Mr. Weasley would be a fine choice for a husband. But I digress. Let me diagram the rock formations on the Smart Board for you."

Dr. Perkins started Smart Boarding. Cashmere turned around and glared at me. *Puhlease!* Like it was my fault she was sleeping through an important class. Far more troubling was who had turned around and was looking at me from the front of the room: Jazmine. And she was grinning.

Nooooo! I had talked my way out of the nurse's office for this? Jazmine. A worthy opponent. Jazmine turned around, flipping her ponytail as she faced the teacher. Her nice, neat ponytail. I put my hand up to my hair and grimaced. Jazmine was wearing a color-block shirt, black pants, and wedges. I had to admit she looked cute, stylish and organized, and put together. I, in my sweats and old T-shirt, looked like I was falling apart.

This was wrong. If Jazmine could be pulled together, so could I.

It was time to regroup. Organize. Prioritize.

Appearance. Superficial, perhaps, but it would help show that I was back in the game. Luckily, I knew Payton always kept a spare outfit in her locker. I'd change into it after class and before my meeting with

Mrs. Burkle. Yep, change of clothes, change of attitude.

Thinking about clothes reminded me of the shopping trip Mom took Payton and me on. We both got dresses for the dance. . . .

"Blah blah blah your homework assignment," Dr. Perkins was saying.

Bzzzt. The bell rang.

Wha—? Class was over? I'd missed the homework assignment! I'd been daydreaming! Me! Spacing out in class?! Oh no. Payton was right. That fall had affected me! My brain was broken.

Onward, Emma. I would start pulling myself together starting *now*. I went to our lockers, but Payton wasn't there. Fortunately, I knew her locker combination. I reached in and pulled out the bag with the extra outfit and her brush. I headed to the nearest bathroom, and a few minutes later, I was in Payton's clothes:

- ✓ Oversized pink sweater (Pink was Payton's signature color, not my favorite, but beggars can't be choosers.)
- ✓ Dark jeans with a little rip in them
- ✓ Brown belt (Boy, Payton was prepared. Accessories and everything.)

The bell rang for next period, just as I brushed my hair and pulled it into a ponytail. There. At least outwardly, I was pulled together. I better get to the classroom where Mrs. Burkle wanted to meet.

"Hi, Emma!" My friend Quinn came down the hall and pushed through the crowd to get near me.

"Hi!" I said. "The hallway looks awesome!" I pointed at the posters on the wall.

"Do you really think they look good?" Quinn worried. "I heard that some people were making fun of the glamorous geckos I drew on them. But I mean, I was trying to put some school spirit into the posters. Go, Geckos, and all that."

"I think they're not only very cute but they're also well drawn," I said emphatically. "I'd never be able to draw lizards in formal wear."

"Thanks, Emma." Quinn lit up. I smiled, because I'd made my friend smile. I was getting much better in the friends/social skills department. "Hey," Quinn said. "Where are you going next?"

"Oh, I have to go see Mrs. Burkle about something," I said. "In the VOGS room. Mrs. Burkle is in that room this period."

"I bet they're interviewing you for VOGS," Quinn

said. "About either your Mathletes win or your TV commercial."

"I hadn't thought about being on camera," I mused. "I was thinking she wanted to talk to me about English homework or something."

Well, it was a good thing I'd changed my clothes. Payton would have to appreciate that. I said good-bye to Quinn and headed toward the VOGS room. I was just about to go in when I noticed the new boy coming around the corner. Just one boy. Still. I was feeling jumpy since the double-triple-vision incident.

Oh no! Another one! I was having another attack of vision problems. *Calm down, Emma,* I told myself. It could be worse. It could be triple vision, like before. And then suddenly, it was. Another new boy. The one boy had turned into three. Three boys coming down the hall.

"Ms. Mills!" Mrs. Burkle's voice rang out. "Time is of the essence! *Entrez vous!*"

I stumbled into the room and blinked to clear my vision. Only one Burkle. Okay, only one. That was good. I looked around. One Nick, standing at a video camera in front of the VOGS set.

Then the new guy entered. Whew! Just one of him.

But wait, he was followed by another one. And another one . . .

"The triplets are here!" Mrs. Burkle announced.

Triplets? TRIPLETS!

Oh. Duh.

I hadn't been seeing triple. Well, I had, but that's because they were triplets! I was an identical twin. You would have thought that I would have figured that one out. But I was thrown off after hitting my head.

Plus, honestly, they did look like one person in triplicate. They were all wearing the same shirt, jeans, and sneakers. They all had black hair cut identically sharp. And when they walked, it was practically in unison.

Even Payton and I weren't like . . . clones.

I watched the three boys as Mrs. Burkle ushered them onto the VOGS set. They were so in sync as they sat down in the chairs, sprawled out, and waited. Were they robots?

"Any questions?" Mrs. Burkle asked them.

"No," they all said, of course, almost at the same time.

"We've been on TV a lot," one of them added. The other two nodded.

"One minute till . . . VOGS showtime!" Mrs. Burkle announced. One minute until VOGS? Why was I here?

Was she going to let me know why she had called me here at this time?

"We're ready!" Burkle waved at me. "Come on over!"

Ready for . . . ?

"What—" I started to say when a girl I didn't know suddenly started attacking the neck of my sweater.

"Shush while I mike you," the girl said clipping a microphone on me. "You'll be heard all over the set. Okay, now say 'Testing, testing.'"

"Testing, testing," I repeated. "But—"

"You know the drill. On set in five." The girl sighed. She practically pushed me onto the set into the seat across from the triplets. "Sometime I hope I get to be on camera too. Payton."

Payton?

"In ten . . ."

Payton!

". . . nine . . ."

They thought I was Payton! I saw the teleprompter angled right at me and I froze. Sure, I'd been on camera in Hollywood, but I had been prepared! I still hated being on camera.

"I think she's nervous," one of the triplets said, grinning.

"Maybe she's never been on camera before," said another one, nodding.

"She can follow our lead," the third said smugly. "Watch and learn."

"I've been on camera!" I started to protest but saw Mrs. Burkle pretending to slice her throat, so I had to stop talking. I took a deep breath and . . . my competitive spirit kicked into gear.

A girl wheeled the teleprompter right in front of me. That's it?

"I just have to read the teleprompter?" I checked.

"Yeah. Since we had to get this on the air so fast, I wrote the news report for you," the girl said. "And three . . . two . . . and you're on the air!"

I looked one of the triplets directly in the eye and smiled my best competition smile. I had a genius IQ—I could read a simple teleprompter! *Don't worry, Payton*, I thought. *I've got this.*

Payton

Seven

BACK TO CLASS . . . AGAIN

I left the principal's office feeling pretty genius. Not like a math genius, but like I'd covered for Principal Patel and Emma pretty well. Just call me mathEmmatician!

Hee!

I practically skipped down the hallway.

I didn't mean to Twin-Switch, but that one couldn't be helped, right? And I had to admit, if we had to have an accidental twin switch, I was glad that it was ME pretending I was Emma, rather than the other way around.

Not that Emma didn't do a good job pretending to be me, I also had to admit. It's just that I preferred to have control over my image. Emma pretending to be me could go smoothly, or it could go very, very wrong.

Eight

BREAKING NEWS

I read my lines off the teleprompter.

"Hi, I'm Payton"—er—I felt a moment of guilt but continued on reading. "Here with a breaking news story. As you may know, I'm an identical twin. And I'm here with three new students who aren't just twins, but triplets!"

The camera flashed to the triplets, who were now smiling.

"I'm Dexter," said one. "That's Oliver and Asher."

Okay, Dexter on the left, Oliver in the middle, Asher on the right. Got it.

"Wow, that is so cool," I read off the teleprompter

and shuddered inwardly. Who wrote these lines? "Are you identical?"

"Yeah," Oliver said. "And identical triplets are extremely rare. One in a million."

"Are you identical?" I read off the teleprompter. Wait. I'd just asked that. It wasn't scrolling ahead.

"Dude," Dexter said. "You just asked us that."

The girl at the teleprompter was shaking it a little bit. Mrs. Burkle had jumped up and was waving her hands in the air, like "keep talking." Oh, great. The teleprompter was stuck, and I had to wing this thing. Okay, keep it rolling. . . .

"Identical triplets *are* extremely rare," I said. "Identical triplets occur when a single fertilized egg splits in two, and then one of the resulting two eggs splits one more time."

There. That should impress them. Except, wait, I was supposed to be Payton. Payton didn't spout facts. I relaxed my shoulders and did my best Payton posture.

"So kewl!" I added.

"Identical triplets are always the same gender and blood type, but they don't have to always look alike," Oliver said.

"But obviously we do," Dexter said.

"Even our parents have trouble telling us apart," Asher said.

"Yeah, my twin and I have that issue," I said.

"Pffft, try being *three*, not just two of you," Dexter said dismissing me.

"Triplets are also called supertwins," Oliver said.

"Super, meaning extraordinary twins, not just regular twins," Dexter said.

Hey, wait a minute. Was that directed at me? It sounded on the surface like he was kidding. But I could tell from my competitions when someone was an opponent.

"Well," I shot back, "everyone is extraordinary in his or her own way. For example, my twin *Emma* has extraordinary talents—"

"And we're really extraordinary because . . ." Dexter said, cutting me off.

"We're the SUPERTWINS!" all three of them said together. And suddenly, in unison, the three of them stood up and faced the camera. The girl who had miked me raced up and handed one a guitar.

"Ah one, two, three," Dexter said.

And they started singing. I looked at Mrs. Burkle, and she looked as surprised as I did.

". . . and ooh, ooh, ooh . . . we're the SuperTwins!"

"We're the SuperTwins!" they said, then gave little waves and sat back down like normal.

The other people in the room started clapping. I looked at Mrs. Burkle, who was beaming and applauding.

"Well, that was unexpected," I said, game face still on. "So you're a boy band?"

"Dude, no." They all shook their heads. "Not a boy band."

"We're a musical force!" Asher added.

"Available for parties, bar and bat mitzvahs . . ." Oliver said.

"Book us now before we hit it big," Dexter said. "Text us."

Mrs. Burkle was making slicing motions across her neck and mouthing something. I was pretty good at reading lips, so I leaned forward. "Wrap it up!" she was saying.

"Well, that's all the time we have," I interrupted them. "Welcome to our school."

I started to get up but nearly strangled myself. The microphone was still attached to my collar. The triplets cracked up.

"Psst! Still rolling!" Mrs. Burkle waved frantically and pointed at the green light, which unfortunately was still on.

". . . and welcome to our school," I added. The green light was still on. Oh, come on, would this never end? The triplets remained slouched in their seats, smirking at me.

"Go, Geckos!" I said weakly.

"And we're off the air!" Mrs. Burkle clapped her hands. "Oh, what I wouldn't give for a higher budget for a new teleprompter. But that was wonderful, triplets. An impromptu musical performance!"

"Thanks," the triplets said in unison. Of course.

"Have you all considered joining the drama club? Or show choir? Are you in band?" Mrs. Burkle tried to enlist them.

"Looks like you all have a lot to chat about, so I'll just be leaving," I said, still in cheery Payton mode. Speaking of which, I needed to get out of there before someone discovered I wasn't Payton. I reached down to detach my mike.

"Can I have your cell? So I can, um, text you guys about playing at a, um, event," the girl who had attached my mike asked. Oh no, their first groupie.

"Tania, please get back to class. Payton, boys, wait while I write you a pass," Mrs. Burkle said.

"Heh, that was funny when she got trapped in the microphone," the triplet in the middle said, elbowing his brothers.

"I wasn't trapped, Oliver," I said pointedly. "Momentarily tangled."

"I'm not Oliver," he smirked.

I looked at the three of them. They must have switched seats.

"And the look on her face when you saw the teleprompter was down," a different one said.

"She was like this." another made a goofy face.

All three triplets made disturbing faces at me. Then laughed. Oh, ha-ha-ha. Yes, something was up with these triplets. On the outside, I was cheerful Payton. On the inside, I was suspicious Emma, checking out the competition. Yes, competition. These guys were trying to make me look bad.

These guys were Triple Trouble.

"*She* is not amused," I told them coolly, finally getting the microphone unhooked from my sweater.

"Oh, admit it, you're our newest superfan," one triplet said.

"Superfan of the SuperTwins," another said. "If you had been nicer to us, we'd have given you our autograph."

"Too bad, so sad," I shot back.

The triplets looked at one another with what I believed was a little surprise. Perhaps they were realizing I was a worthy opponent. I was not going to let their little mind games get to me. Good thing it was me, Emma, and not Payton here. I'd faced down every type of competitor in existence: intimidators, scrappers, come-from-behinders . . . I wasn't about to be taken down by boy banders!

"Hey, do you think she . . . ?" one of the triplets said cryptically.

The other two laughed.

"Agreed," one said.

"Eh, maybe," said the third.

What the—? Were they having a conversation? They were all quiet, and then they burst out laughing.

"Are you feeling left out?" one of the triplets said to me.

"We're just having a little triplet talk," one said.

"But you weren't talking," I pointed out.

One of the triplets grinned and leaned back in his chair with the front feet off the floor.

"Well, you know how some multiples can read one another's minds—" he said.

"—and finish one another's sentences," another said.

"That's a myth," I pointed out. "We can be attuned to each other, but not really read each others' minds."

"Whatever you say," one triplet said and shrugged. The other two laughed.

"Vanilla," one suddenly said.

"Agreed," the other answered.

Wait. Were they really reading one another's minds? No. Of course not. ESP was scientifically impossible.

"Twelve," the other said. "Definitely."

No. There was no way. The triplets stood up at exactly the same time. But these *super*Twins weren't *super*natural. Scientifically. Impossible. Okay, that was a little eerie.

I had to admit, I'd always been irritated by the question, "Can you and your twin read each other's minds?" There was absolutely no evidence of telepathic communication between twins. There were times when Payton and I did seem attuned to each other in ways that seemed to defy science. But that, of course, was because we lived together, went to the same school, looked almost exactly alike . . .

Then I noticed that the triplets were eyeing me up and down.

"Hey, Payton?" one of the triplets said.

"Come closer. We want tell you apart from your sister," one of the triplets said.

"We know how annoying some multiples get when people mix you up," the third said.

"Look at the time," I said. "I have to get to class!"

I fled.

Payton

Nine

FOURTH PERIOD

Clothes? Meat? Flowers?

I only had a couple more minutes to get to my locker, find my social studies textbook, and find out what the last two exports were. . . .

When I got to my locker, it was buzzing. I'd forgotten to turn off my cell phone. I opened the door and grabbed my cell to see who was texting me during a school day.

Emma? Why was Emma texting me? I clicked on it. *JC! NOW!*

The Janitor's Closet? Emma wanted me to meet her at the Janitor's Closet? The site of our Twin Switches? Did Emma want to switch places?

That was a coincidence, since I'd just pretended I was Emma in the principal's office. It was definitely a TWINcidence. Identical twins have a lot of coincidences! Like the famous story our parents told us about these real-life identical twins who were separated at birth. They met when they were grown-up and found out that their adoptive parents named them both James! And the men had each married women named Linda, and they named their sons James and their dogs Toy!

Weird!

I walked quickly to the Janitor's Closet. We had only ten minutes before next period, and I didn't want to be late to social studies. I turned the corner and—

"Hey!"

Emma grabbed me and practically shoved me into the closet. *Bzzzt!*

"What the heck?" I hissed. A tiny light flicked on.

"Hurry! Switch clothes with me!" Emma said. "We can see by the light of my prizewinning flashlight/pen/key chain."

Bzzzt!

"Switch outfits?" I protested. "I like my outfit today. Ow!"

Emma had accidentally elbowed me as she pulled off a pink sweater. Hey, wait a minute.

"Are you wearing my sweater?" I peered closer.

"Yes, and your jeans and belt," Emma grumbled. "I got them from your locker. We need to switch clothes so we're not busted."

Ah, she must have found out about my awesome performance as MathEmmatician in the principal's office. I opened my mouth to boast about it just as the first warning bell for class rang. We could hear the rush of our classmates right outside the door.

I shut my mouth. We didn't want anyone to discover our JC switching place, that's for sure. I tried not to yelp as we bumped into each other. It was a teeny closet. Good thing the janitor had the mop and the bucket out or we wouldn't have fit. I pulled the sweater on. At least she had the decency to have me switch into cute clothes and not the heinous outfit she'd had on this morning, with the green scrunchie.

"Ready!" I whispered to Emma. Emma opened the door a teeny tiny bit. We could see the madhouse of kids walking in the halls. Emma slid out. I crossed my fingers that nobody had noticed her.

I waited. Five . . . four . . . three . . . two . . . one. Then I slipped out of the closet and tried to blend in with the crowd. I blended, but got swept along with the tide of kids rushing to their next class. Where was Emma? I wanted to fill her in on what just happened. I tried to look around the person in front of me to find my sister.

"Hey, watch out." It was Sydney.

"Sydney, do you see Emma?" I hated to ask her for any help, but I needed to find out why we just switched clothes.

"No, I see Payton," she said, looking at me. "I think, anyway. Unless you're Emma and you're looking for yourself."

"Ha, very funny," I said. "Twin humor. Ha."

"You guys are old news anyway." She shrugged. "They're so cool, you know?"

Before I could ask her what she was talking about, she pushed forward into the crowd. Then I spotted Emma.

Excellent!

Except as I got closer, I realized that Emma was talking to her science teacher.

Not so excellent. I wanted to fill Emma in on what had happened in the principal's office. I waited for a minute, trying to use twin ESP to get Emma's attention.

"Emma! Stop talking to your science teacher and talk to me!" I tried to tell her silently. But Emma not only didn't stop talking to the teacher, she got even more animated, waving her hands around.

She must be talking about sciencey things only Emma would get excited about. Then the second warning bell rang. Shoot, I was going to be late for social studies.

I hurried through the hall. I noticed people looking at someone, and I saw the new guy coming down the hall toward me.

"Hi," I said to him. I knew it must be weird to be the new guy. He looked at me and didn't say anything. Well, yeesh. He could have at least acknowledged my presence, after trying to make me do his math for him.

I ran down the stairs.

"Hi, Payton!" Tess waved as she went by.

"Hey there, Payton," the new guy said—smirking?— as he went . . . up the stairs? Wait a minute. How did the new guy get there so fast? And this time he said hi to me. My head was spinning as I got to social studies just as the bell rang and slid into my seat.

"Please pass your homework forward," Mr. Schain said.

As I passed my paper forward, the principal's voice came over the loudspeaker.

"We will have a special breaking-news VOGS update," the principal said. "Please turn on your classroom televisions for this news."

"This is going to delay our lesson on the triangular trade route," Mr. Schain grumbled and turned on the television.

"Hello, Geckos," Ahmad, one of the VOGS reporters, came on-screen. "We have a special news update. The parking lot will unexpectedly be closed off for paving. Seniors, if you park in Lot B, move, or you could be towed away by quarter past eleven. Also the faculty parking lot, too. So. Teachers. Move your cars. Thank you."

"Great," Mr. Schain grumbled. "Just great."

As Mr. Schain was pulling his keys out of his desk drawer, Mrs. Burkle's face came on-screen.

"And while we have a captive audience, let's add on a feature report!" Mrs. Burkle looked thrilled. She loved being able to, as she put it, "break into regularly scheduled classes."

And then something weird happened. Emma's face came on the television. WHAT?!

"Hi, I'm Payton," Emma said.

Emma say what? Why was Emma on VOGS saying she was me? People turned around to look at me. Heh. I smiled weakly and tried not to freak out. I kept my eyes glued to the screen.

"As you may know, I'm an identical twin," Emma

was saying. "And I'm here with three new students who aren't just twins, but triplets!"

And the camera panned to the new guy. And the new guy and the . . . Ohhh! Suddenly things made sense. The new guy didn't move really fast! He was a triplet!

Now I realized why we had to switch clothes. Emma was on VOGS being me, wearing my pink sweater, which I was in now. Wait, why was she being me in the first place? Why wasn't I being me? Oh . . . it must have been while *I* was being *her* in the principal's office!

OMIgosh! Accidental Twin Switch!

"Are you identical?" Emma said, obviously reading off the teleprompter. Ugh. If she was going to impersonate me, she needed to do a better job of not so obviously reading. I mean, I did a fabulous job being her in the principal's office. She could return the favor.

Then I thought about how I'd flipped my hair and done "Shiny, shiny, shiny" to the school board. Maybe I'd cut Emma some slack on the teleprompter thing.

We all watched with fascination as the triplets introduced themselves. Dexter, Oliver, Asher. They really, really looked identical. It was so cool! I tried to tell them apart, but they were dressed alike and sounded alike.

Whenever I met other identicals, I realized how

other people looked at Emma and me. Like right now, everyone was watching Emma on-screen, thinking she was me. She was doing a good job now, though. She looked like she wasn't even reading the teleprompter. I relaxed a little bit. She was being me pretty good!

Then things got unusual. The triplets started to sing.

"Oooh!" a girl squealed. "We have a new boy band in our school!"

I leaned forward, trying to watch and see what Emma/I was saying. But the class got so noisy.

"They're so cute!" girls were saying.

"Seriously?" one guy snorted.

"You're just jealous," a girl said. "You wish you were an identical adorable triplet guy musician."

I couldn't hear what was happening on VOGS. What was Emma saying? Why were the triplets smirking at her? My class finally quieted down just as the interview was ending.

"Go, Geckos!" Emma said. And did her awkward fist punch in the air.

Sigh.

Well, I'd unraveled the mystery of the new guys(s). Now I needed to unravel the mystery of why Emma had been filming VOGS while I'd been answering math questions.

Emma

Ten

AT LUNCH

I left my class.

Ox was there waiting for me. He looked very cute. But not very pleased. He arched an eyebrow at me.

"I can explain," I said immediately.

"You can explain why you impersonated your sister for the VOGS cast?" Ox asked. "I thought you two were done switching places so you wouldn't get into any more trouble."

"I know." I nodded. We walked together down the hall, and I explained what happened.

"So I didn't know that I was *doing* the interviewing as Payton. I thought I was *being* interviewed as Emma.

So, as you can see, I had no other alternative," I said to close my argument.

"You couldn't just have said, 'I'm Emma, there's been a mistake?'" he asked.

I Hmmm . . . good question. I stopped and moved off to the side where we wouldn't get plowed over by people on their way to class.

"Okay," I confessed. "The triplets threw me off my game, and I got flustered."

Ox arched his eyebrow again.

"And then they started challenging me, and—okay—I started getting competitive." I sighed. "Like animals that instinctively guard their own territory?" Ox smiled. He was an animal activist as well as an athlete.

"Well, that's honest," Ox said. "I get that."

"I may have handled it wrong," I admitted. "Can I blame it on my bumped head? This day has been ridiculous."

"Yeah, I was worried about you, " Ox said, his face changing to a look of concern. "Are you okay?"

Then Ox put his arm around me.

OX PUT HIS ARM AROUND ME! Was I okay? I was more than okay because OX HAD HIS ARM AROUND ME!

Now I was feeling flustered for sure. "Flustered" was definitely the accurate word for it.

Tee hee hee.

The warning bell for class rang.

"Well, I better get to PE," Ox said. "Need to keep in shape for football. And our dance."

Tee hee—erp. Our dance. I'd conveniently forgotten about that part.

"I better get to lunch," I said. "Need to . . . uh . . ."

"Eat?" Ox finished the sentence for me. He took his arm back, and I came to my senses and said good-bye.

I went to my locker, and Payton was standing there waiting for me.

"You could have told me you pretended to be me for VOGS," she whisper-hissed to me.

"I thought I'd have plenty of time," I said. "I thought it would air at the end of school, not in the middle of it!"

"Still," Payton said, arms crossed. "You should have told me in the JC."

"I thought it was more important for us to change so we didn't get busted," I said. "Then we had to be silent, remember? Then I ran into my science teacher, and I had to ask her about the homework assignment. . . ."

"Next time, before any of that, you need to tell me

that you JUST PRETENDED TO BE ME!" Payton's voice rose. People turned to look at her, and her cheeks turned pinker than the sweater we'd both worn. She lowered her voice. "I need to be prepared. Everyone is asking me about the triplets, and I have to fake knowing something."

"I don't know much more than what you saw on VOGS," I said. Then I lowered my voice even more. "But it was a little odd. They kept making comments about triplets being better than twins."

"To you?" Payton asked. I nodded.

"And there was something else odd," I mused. "I know it sounds ridiculous, but they seemed to be talking to one another in, well, twin ESP. I mean, triplet ESP."

"But you don't believe in any of that!" Payton said. "Maybe they were lip-reading like you tried to do for your failed science project."

"It wasn't a *failed* project. Jazmine protested it before I even made it, that's all," I said, scowling. "Anyway their lips weren't moving. Like I said, it was all very strange."

The warning bell rang. The hallway got loud as students raced to their classes.

"Eeps! I forgot to tell *you* something," Payton said, slamming her locker door. "While you were being me, I was being you. I had to do a Mathletes demonstration in the principal's office for the school board."

"You *what*?!" My jaw dropped.

"Don't worry. I was great," Payton said. "Have to go or I'll be late to class. Bye!"

But . . . but . . . I watched my sister hurry away. I thought about what a Mathletes demonstration by Payton would be, and shuddered. On second thought, I didn't want to think about it at all.

I had lunch this period. Although I wasn't hungry (third-period lunch), I knew I'd need sustenance to get through this kind of day. I grabbed my lunch bag and headed into the cafeteria.

"Hi, Emma!" Tess said.

I sat down next to her, in my usual seat between her and Courtney Jones.

"I was just saying how I have two of those triplets in my gym class," Courtney said. "Cashmere tried to talk them into singing for us, but they said they only perform when they're all together. And for money. I think that was a joke."

I wouldn't be so sure. Those triplets were a little slick.

"They look so much alike," Tess said. "Don't you think, Emma?"

"Definitely," I said.

"I wish I had a twin or triplet." Courtney sighed. "Well, at least I have quintuplet hamster babies."

Courtney was pretty into her hamsters. I'd first met her at a science fair, when her hamster had gotten loose from an exhibit. She was a contender this year for a prize, but my fiercest competition was, of course, Jazmine.

Jazmine James, who was walking by my lunch table with Hector. And stopping.

"Guess what, Emma and Courtney?" Jazmine said. "I got the final phase of my science project approved this morning."

"It's outstanding," Hector added.

"How's your science project coming?" Jazmine asked.

"So great!" Courtney said. "I'm getting some interesting results about the effects of music on hamsters. I'm testing whether or not they run faster on their wheels to different kinds of music."

"I hope you're not set up next to me," Jazmine said. "Hamsters creep me out."

"They're cute and fuzzy," Tess said, jumping to Courtney's defense. "I think it's an interesting idea."

"Emma," Jazmine said turning to me. "You're so lucky. You must have *so* much free time, while the rest of us slave away at our science fair projects."

"Oh, I have a lot going on. You know, special projects and all that," I said breezily. Before I could change the direction of this conversation to a discussion of our English paper (A+!), it was changed for me.

"It's Emma!" a voice yelled across the cafeteria. "We want to sit with Emma!"

The entire cafeteria turned to see who was yelling. It was Jason, with Mason and their mother, Counselor Case. The boys were carrying lunch trays. And they were heading my way.

"Looks like you have some groupies." Jazmine smirked and walked off with Hector in tow.

"Sorry in advance for this," I told Tess and Courtney.

"Oh, I think they're adorable!" Tess said.

"Almost as cute as my hamsters," Courtney said.

"Yeah, they are," I agreed. "But they're more unpredictable than hamsters."

"Emma, guess what? We're here for lunch!" Mason and Jason ran up to me, their lunch trays precariously balanced. "Can we sit with you?"

Counselor Case hurried over.

"Boys, let Emma have her lunch in peace," she said, and turned to me. "Sorry. The boys have a two-hour delay at the elementary school. We're killing time."

"They can sit with me," I told Counselor Case. I actually enjoyed Mason and Jason—most of the time. Plus, they just got rid of Jazmine James, so I felt like I owed them one. I slid over so they could sit on my bench.

"Do you mind if I run to the office?" Counselor Case said. "I'll be back in just a few minutes."

"No problem," I said as she left.

"Emma, did you see those new triplets?" Jason asked me. "They were in Mom's office this morning with us."

"They look a lot alike, don't they?" I asked them, unwrapping my tuna sandwich and carefully setting the pickle I'd packed to the side.

"They have magic powers," Mason added, digging into his hot-lunch mac and cheese. "They showed us."

"Not magic," Jason scoffed. "Telepathy. And telepathy isn't scientifically proven. But . . . it was spooky."

I thought about what the triplets had done after the interview.

"What did they do?" Tess was fascinated.

"They said they read one another's minds," Jason said, popping a chicken nugget in his mouth. "They showed us. They had a whole conversation without words."

Hmmm. It *was* interesting what the triplets had done earlier too. While Payton and I couldn't really read each other's minds, I often did think I knew what she was thinking. And I thought about the coincidences—twin-cidences—that Payton and I had.

"I bet we can do that," Mason was saying. "Jase, think of something and I'll tell you what it is."

Jason stared at Mason.

"You're thinking . . ." Mason paused and put his hands to his forehead. "You're thinking that Emma's friends are cute."

"I was not!" Jason jumped up, his face red.

Mason raised an eyebrow.

"Mason," I warned, "be nice to your brother."

"Let's see if he can read your mind," Courtney said. "For real, though."

"Okay," Jason stared at Mason.

"He's thinking that his mac and cheese is gross," Jason said.

"Yeah!" Mason's eyes widened. "I was. How did you do that?"

"Really? Do you think you read his mind?" Tess asked.

"I don't know," Jason said. "It just popped into my head."

"It might be the nonverbal signals," I pointed out.

"You may have seen Mason grimace, indicating he wasn't enjoying his food."

"No, I'm the psychic twin," Jason said. "Mason's just psycho."

Mason stuck out his tongue. It was covered in mac and cheese. Gross.

"Easy, guys," I said. I took a bite out of my apple.

"Try to read my mind again then," Mason challenged Jason.

The two boys stared at each other. And stared.

"Why aren't you saying anything?" Mason challenged.

"Your brain is empty," Jason said. "As usual."

"Hey!" Mason said. Before we could stop him, he reached into Jason's mac and cheese with his hand and squished it around.

"Boys!" I said. "Cut it—"

"Hey!" Jason protested. He knocked Mason's hand away, and the goo from the mac and cheese flew off Mason's hand and sprayed us all.

"What the—" a voice behind us yelped. I turned around to see that Hector had mac and cheese in his hair too.

"Ew, Hector," Jazmine said, leaning away from him. But unfortunately for her, she leaned closer to our table just as Jason threw a chicken nugget at Mason. However, Jason wasn't known for his aim. The nugget flew past Mason and landed on Jazmine's table.

"AUH!" Jazmine screeched as ketchup splatted her.

"Woo yah! Food fight!" Mason yelled.

"No, no." I tried to shush him. But it was too late. The words had been spoken.

"Food fight!" Someone took up the rallying cry.

Duck and cover! Duck and cover! I started to slide under the table, but it was too late. Splat! A piece of lettuce splatted on my cheek. Salad dressing dripped down onto my (Payton's) sweater.

"Food fight!" people were yelling.

Chaos! Yelling! Squealing! And then a piece of lunch meat flew over my head. Food was flying everywhere!

"Boys!" Mason and Jason were winging mac and cheese and nuggets. Please tell me I can't be held responsible for this, can I? I grasped each boy by the neck and lifted them like kittens.

"Read my mind, guys," I growled at them.

"But that's scientifically impos—" Jason protested.

"Guess!" I cut him off, dragging both of them away from the table.

"Stop throwing food?" Jason asked.

"And get out of here?" Mason asked.

"Exactly," I said. "Let's go find your mother."

We maneuvered around the tables and the cafeteria aides trying to avoid the flying food and get to the door. Counselor Case rushed in just as we reached it.

"What on earth is going—?" Counselor Case started to say, but didn't get to finish. Because a carton of chocolate milk flew past her, spraying her from head to toes.

"Awes—" Mason started to say, but Jason read his mind.

"—ful," Jason elbowed him. "That's just awful."

Good save, Jason.

Payton

Eleven

AT DINNER

"So Counselor Case tried to blot the chocolate milk off, but it was fruitless," Emma said as she reached over and plucked the last of the chow mein fun with her chopsticks.

We were finishing dinner at our favorite Chinese restaurant. Emma was filling us in on the details of the epic food fight at lunch. It was the only time I'd ever wished I'd had third-period lunch.

"I remember this food fight I was in once," my dad said looking gleeful. "It was spaghetti day at school, and the principal walked in just as I was throwing a plate and—"

"Ahem," my mother said. "Don't be a bad influence on the girls."

"And that's my cue to pay the bill," Dad said, cheerfully sliding out of the booth and heading up to the front room where the cashier was located.

"You're so lucky," I grumbled. "I've never been in a food fight."

"Now, that's something to be *proud* of," my mother told me. "Although Emma, I'm glad you helped Counselor Case."

"Well, it worked out great for me," Emma said. "Because as punishment, the twins have to do an extra day with me."

"That *is* punishment, spending extra time with you," I snorted.

Emma shot me a look.

"I'm getting paid extra money too," she said. "So, ha!"

"Don't forget your fortune cookies," the server said as she came up and placed four of them on a silver tray. She looked at me and then at Emma and then back at me. I knew what she was thinking.

"Yes, we're twins," I told her. "Identical."

"I see it's a night for that," the server said. "You should see the three twins in the front room. They look even more alike than you too!"

I guess I didn't know what she was thinking after all.

"Three twins?" my mom asked. "Triplets?"

Emma and I looked at each other. We hadn't mentioned the new triplets to our parents yet. We'd talked about it when we had gotten home. I told Emma I wasn't going to say anything, because I was afraid I'd blurt out something stupid about VOGS and Emma being me. Emma said she didn't want to say anything, because she didn't want to judge them yet on their first day.

(But she thought they'd been mean.)

"Oh, yeah," Emma said. "I forgot to tell you. There are new identical triplets in school. Boys. They have their own boy band too."

"Neat," my mom said. "Did you meet them?"

"Yeeesss," we both said slowly. We were saved from answering any more by our dad, who had come back to the table.

"Maybe we can sneak out. You hide behind Mom, and I'll hide behind Dad," I whispered to Emma, who nodded.

"Hey, guess what?" Dad said to us. "I just bumped into some triplets, and when I mentioned I, too, had identicals, they said they go to your school. Come and say hello."

"What a coincidence!" my mom said.

"A twincidence?" I whispered to Emma. "Or what would you call a triplet-coincindence?"

"Annoying," Emma muttered back. "I'd call it annoying. They're everywhere."

Emma and I followed Dad out to the front room. Yup, the triplets were there, sitting with two women who looked like—each other.

"This is my wife, and these are my twins." Dad nudged us closer to the table.

"I'm Bonita, and this is *my* twin sister, Belinda," the woman said. "And these are my sons, Dexter, Oliver, and Asher."

I couldn't tell which one went with which name.

"We met in school," I said. "Hi, I'm Payton. That's Emma."

"One of them interviewed us, and the other one was lying on the floor in a hallway," a triplet said.

Our parents looked at us.

"We didn't get to tell you guys about the rest of our day," I said brightly.

"So many stories, not enough time," Emma added, even more brightly.

"Just to be sure, which one of you is which?" I asked them. "I know how annoying it can be when people just lump you together because you look alike."

"Dexter is the charmer, Oliver is the funny one, and

Asher is the sensitive one whose thoughts run deep," the mother said.

"Oh, how . . . interesting," my mom said, looking slightly flustered.

"The boys formed a music group, so you know how it is," their mother said. "These days they need a brand, which, of course, in our case is triplets."

"SuperTwins," a triplet nodded.

"But each boy needs to have his own identity," their mother said.

"Oh, I highly agree," my mom said. "It's important for multiples to feel like individuals."

"Actually, I meant for marketing purposes," their mother chuckled. "Like Paul was the cute one, Ringo was the funny one, George was the quiet one . . . You want to have a member to appeal to different girls."

"Oh." my father said. There was a moment of quiet.

"Well, welcome, and I hope you're enjoying your new community and school," my mom said cheerily.

"Thank you," Bonita said. "We're celebrating the boys' first day at school after our move here. I just divorced their father, and we moved in with Belinda."

That could be hard, a divorce and a move. I smiled at the triplets to show that I was understanding of that. They just eyed me back, without any facial expression at all. *Okay.*

"Of course, eventually we plan to end up in LA or New York or Nashville for the business, so it's temporary," their mother continued.

My parents just nodded.

"So you two are twin sisters?" Emma asked. "The prevalence of multiples in family histories interests me."

"Yes, Belinda and I are identical twins, just like you girls," the mother said. "Obviously, multiples run in our family."

"I'm so pleased that Bonita and the boys will be here for the festival," Belinda said.

"What festival?" my mom asked.

"The annual multiples fest: Multipalooza," Bonita said. "A festival to celebrate multiples. Belinda is on the board of directors for it. You must bring the girls!"

"This year the boys will get to attend for the first time," Belinda said. "It was previously for adults. But now we're having a new Multiples Tweens and Teens division."

"You've never seen so many identicals in your life!" Bonita said.

A whole festival just for twins and supertwins! I did want to go! Emma and I would be among our people! I wondered what we should wear. Should we dress alike? Or not exactly alike, just complement each other with coordinating colors and—

"And there will be all kinds of competitions," Belinda added.

I saw Emma perk up at that.

"The boys will be performing this year," Bonita said.

"It's about a two-hour drive from here," Belinda was saying to my parents. "It's Saturday, the—"

"Not the dance weekend, I hope," I blurted out.

"Oh, is there a dance?" Belinda asked the triplets.

"Yeah, a homecoming thing," one of the triplets answered. "All these girls were asking us to go with them. They saw us on that video show at school and came after us."

These guys should call themselves the Super*Ego* twins. Ha. I bet Emma would be proud of me for that joke.

"We can text you the details about Multipalooza," Bonita said.

"Great, what's your cell?" Emma asked.

"I don't have a new one yet, so boys, one of you text Emma your number, please," she said.

One of them did, although he didn't look too happy about it. We said good-bye to Belinda and Bonita.

"Bye, Dexter, Oliver, and Asher," Emma said to the triplets. They gave us a forced good-bye back.

"Can we go to the multiples festival? Can we go?" Emma said, as we went out the door and into the parking lot.

"I don't know," my mom said. "It seems like a little too much. A festival and a dance."

"I'm *definitely* going to the dance," I warned. Definitely. (With Nick!)

"Well, I *definitely* want to go to the festival now," Emma said excitedly. "I've been craving competition."

Emma was practically skipping.

"It would be nice to go somewhere where we're not so unusual," I said. "Where we fit in. Where everyone looks like someone."

"That does make a compelling argument," Dad said.

"I think it would be fun," I agreed. "All those twins and triplets and quads? Pretty cool."

"I have to admit, it sounds like fun," my mom said, nodding. "Okay, I think it's a good idea."

"On one condition," my dad said. "You're not going as a brand, a package, or to be marketed. Deal?"

"Deal!" Emma and I said at the same time. I smiled at Emma. Sometimes it was fun being a twin.

"We'll just be us," Emma reassured our dad.

We gave each other a twin hand-clap-slap. We were going to Multipalooza!

Emma

Twelve

LATER THAT WEEK, AFTER SCHOOL

After last period, I stopped at my locker and headed to the library for my tutoring session.

"Hi, Emma," Ox said. He was leaning against the wall just outside the library.

"Hi!" I said. "What are you doing here?"

"Well, I knew you had tutoring today, and I've got a few minutes to kill before I suit up for football practice, so I hoped I'd get to see you." Ox smiled.

I smiled.

Ox smiled.

"Um, so." I tried to continue the conversation. "Does football season last all year?"

Ox snorted.

"Actually, football is a fall sport," he told me. "We only have one more game."

"Oh!" I thought fast. "That gives your team one last chance to get over .500! Or, conversely, if you lost, your percentage would only be .416 repeating six. That's not so good."

"Yeah," Ox agreed. "But I had one hundred percent fun playing, and I think next year our team will be really good. I'm moving up to junior varsity. They play on the high school field, so it'll be cool. You'll have to come cheer me on."

"Me?" I cringed, imagining myself in a cheer outfit attempting clumsy cartwheels.

"Only if you want to," Ox said quickly. "I know sitting in the stands isn't exactly thrilling. . . ."

"Oh! In the stands!" I started laughing. "I thought you expected me to be a cheerleader!"

"Only in your dreams, Twin," Sydney said, passing by holding pom-poms. "Cheerleading is for the athletic and adorable. Not mathletic and dork-able."

"Very clever, Sydney. Ha-ha!" I said. Insulting, but clever. I remembered back when Sydney had wanted Ox to be *her* boyfriend, but instead he liked ME. Ha-ha.

"I was just kidding!" She smiled at Ox.

"Saying 'just kidding' doesn't excuse an insult," Ox told her. Then he turned to me. "Though it's not really an insult because I like mathletic and dorkable."

I swooned. Sydney flounced off. Ha-ha.

"Emma! I got a new geometry app for my phone!" Jason came running down the hall toward us, followed by Mason and Counselor Case.

"That's *my* cell phone, Jason," Counselor Case corrected him.

"And I made slime in science today! Wanna see?" Mason held out an orange blob.

"Great," I said.

"Cool, dude," Ox said.

"Just to be clear, that does not go in my hair or in my tote bag," I informed Mason.

"Aw." Mason's face dropped.

"Emma, before you begin with the boys, I wanted to update you on the plans for the Multipalooza festival," Counselor Case said.

"We're going too!" Mason and Jason screamed and jumped around like crazy people.

"Ox, can you come?" Mason stopped jumping. He treated Ox like a hero, which was pretty cute.

"He can't come," Jason scoffed. "He's just a singleton."

"JUST a singleton?" Ox frowned. "JUST?" He reached down and picked Jason up off the ground. Then he pulled Mason up too.

"Just ONE of me can lift TWO of you," he said while the twins dangled from his arms, giggling.

Ox let Mason and Jason down. Then he looked at me. "I should get to practice," he said. "What's this festival?"

"And I have some math tutoring to do," I said.

Jason cheered and Mason groaned.

"I'll call you after dinner," Ox told me, and said good-bye to everyone.

"Oooh, I know math," Mason said. "Ox plus Emma equals L-U-V . . ."

"Enough, Mason," Counselor Case said. "Boys, behave yourselves with Emma. I'll see you at five o'clock."

As I herded the twins through the library doors, Jason said, "Actually, did you know that Ox plus Emma results in Oxemma, which is a patented health care technology used for diagnostic imaging?"

Mason and I were silent.

Oxemma? Hee.

"Time for math," I said firmly. I had a job to do.

I could think about Ox later.

Hee.

Thirteen

VOGS MEETING

I sat in the VOGS meeting, waiting in suspense. Mrs. Burkle was giving out assignments for the next session of VOGS. Oh, how I hoped I would be an anchor and get to introduce the show! I thought I'd proved myself pretty well lately. I had been doing short news stories the past few weeks and wanted something juicier.

"Our anchors will be . . ." We all held our breath. Then she announced four people who were . . . not me. Rats. I let out my breath. I'd really been hoping. I saw Nick shoot me a glance of pity. I tried to put a smile on my face like it was no big deal. After the meeting ended, Nick came right over.

"Hey, I'm sorry," Nick said. "I know you wanted to be an anchor.

"Oh, it's no big deal," I said.

Nick looked at me.

"Oh, okay, it is a big deal," I confessed.

"Why don't you go ask Mrs. Burkle about it?" Nick asked. "Not to complain, just to ask if there's something you can do to get the anchor spot next time."

"Well." I looked over and saw that Burkle was standing by herself.

"I have to grab something from my locker, but text me how it goes," Nick said. "See you."

I said bye to Nick, then took a deep breath and approached Burkle.

"Mrs. Burkle?" I asked her. "I'm not complaining, but I was wondering if there is something I can do differently so I can be an anchor next time?"

"Oh, Payton, I'm glad to see you express an interest. Well, I did just give you the plum interview opportunity for the breaking-news feature, interviewing the triplets."

Ergh. I couldn't tell her that was Emma, not me! It was so unfair!

"A little constructive criticism: The interview was a little choppy," Mrs. Burkle said. "I'd like you to work on your closures and also looking at the camera more."

ERGH! Now it was REALLY unfair! I was being judged for Emma's work! Nooooo!

"May I have a chance to show you I can do better?" I practically begged.

"Well, I am looking for exciting features. The triplets story did generate a lot of interest. Perhaps we can pursue that further?"

"I have an idea," I said. "I'm going to a multiples festival! I can report from there."

"Well, I was thinking more of an in-depth interview with our own students," Mrs. Burkle said.

"Well, the triplets *will* be there," I said. "Their aunt is one of the people who runs it. And Emma and I are both going. We could have our first VOGS on location!"

"We haven't gone on location before." Mrs. Burkle looked thoughtful.

I held my breath. It would be like I was a real news reporter, reporting news from exotic places all over the world. It would almost be like having my own show.

"Didn't you say you're looking for exciting ways to expand VOGS, right?" I asked her.

"That is very true!" Mrs. Burkle nodded. "I think it's an idea worth exploring further. Bring me a plan. Dates, times, students' names, story ideas. I'll ask the principal about field trip permissions, liabilities, logistics, and chaperones."

"Okay!" I nodded so hard I thought my head would fall off.

This would be awesome. I'd be the first traveling news correspondent for VOGS! If I could prove myself, Burkle would have to let me be the anchor next semester, wouldn't she?

"I'll head straight to the principal's office to propose this. I have some boxes to bring there anyway. Would you kindly assist me?" Burkle asked.

"Sure. I'm going that way anyway to catch the late bus," I told her. She handed me a filing box, and we walked down the hallway.

"So Emma and I will go. And the triplets. Also, would it be okay if I could pick the cameraperson for the segment?" I asked her.

"Perhaps are you referring to Nicholas?" Burkle smiled knowingly.

I felt myself turn red. Even the teachers knew we liked each other?

"I'll put Nick on the request list," Burkle said.

We walked down the stairs, and I heard some familiar voices echoing down the hall. It was Mason and Jason.

As I turned the corner, I could see that Emma was walking with them toward the main office door. That's where Counselor Case had her office.

"Hey, it's Payton! And hi, English teacher lady!" Mason yelled. "Hey, Payton! Guess what? We were guinea pigs!"

Mason crouched down on the floor and pretended to be a guinea pig.

"Although we didn't have conclusive results," Jason said. "Right, Emma? Right, Emma?"

Emma looked pained. "We were learning about probability," she said. "So I had them do an experiment on the odds of one of them reading the other's mind. Purely unscientific, of course."

"How did it go?" Mrs. Burkle asked.

"Wheeet! Wheeet!" Mason did what I think was supposed to be a guinea pig noise imitation. "We beat the odds."

"We had seventy-four percent accuracy!" Jason said.

"What does that mean?" I asked.

"Nothing," Emma grumbled. "It was just a game."

"It means we have twin ESP!" Mason whooped and stood up. "E! S! P! E! S! P!" he chanted.

"And it means I have a headache," Emma groaned,

putting her hand to her forehead. "Hi, Mrs. Burkle."

"Boys, would you chivalrously hold the door for us since our hands are full?" Mrs. Burkle asked. Jason pushed the door open, and we all walked in.

I put the box down where Mrs. Burkle set hers just as Counselor Case came out.

"Hello, Bertha. Hey, gang. I thought I heard my sweet boys," Counselor Case said. "They *were* sweet for you, Emma, weren't they?"

"I can answer that! I can read Emma's mind," Jason said. "She's thinking no! Mason was *not* sweet, but Jason was."

"Nuh-uh," Mason said. "She's thinking Mason is sweeeeet. And better-looking."

"Yes, that's exactly what I was thinking," Emma sighed. "You both do have ESP. I don't need to do any further experiments."

"I knew it!" the boys said.

"I think she was being sarcastic," Counselor Case said.

"This sounds like a fascinating experiment," Mrs. Burkle said. "It could make a good news story for VOGS as a follow-up story to our trip to the Multipalooza."

"The twins and multiples festival?" Counselor Case asked.

"Yes, I'm proposing that VOGS travel to the festival next weekend to tape a feature," Mrs. Burkle said.

"I'd love to hear more about this," Counselor Case said. "Is it for kids?"

"Yeah, they have a kids division," I said. Then I caught Emma's face. Oops. Maybe I shouldn't have mentioned that.

"Wonderful! Coach and I will have to bring the boys," Counselor Case said.

"Fabulous, and we can feature Mason and Jason in the VOGS cast," Mrs. Burkle said. "We can show older twins mentoring younger twins."

"Perhaps we can all caravan together," Counselor Case said.

"I want to ride in a car with Emma!" Jason said. "We can do spelling bee words the whole way."

"*I* call sitting next to Emma," Mason said. "Can I bring Mascot?"

"I need to get out of here," Emma whispered to me in a strangled voice.

Emma was Mason'd and Jason'd out, that was for sure.

"Look at the time!" Emma said. "Payton and I need to catch our late bus. So, bye, everyone!"

"Maybe Emma can sit in between us on the ride,"

Jason was saying. "If we take Dad's car, it's real squishy in the back. Emma can sit on the hump!"

"Flee," Emma said under her breath. And we fled.

"Sorry about that," I said to Emma as we headed down the hallway.

"Oh, you know I like Mason and Jason," Emma said. "In small doses. Chaperoned by their parents. Without a gecko. And if possible, fifty feet away from me."

We walked into the school lobby, Emma pausing for a moment as always in front of the trophy booth to see her name on some of the trophies.

"Hi, Emma!" Nick came into the lobby too. "So, Payton, how did it go?"

"I'll let you two chat," Emma said. "I'm going to go to the bus and make sure I get my front seat."

"See you in a minute," I said to her. Then I turned to Nick. "It went great. Thanks so much for making me talk to Burkle."

I told him about my idea for Multipalooza.

"Cool," he said, looking impressed.

"So, um . . ." I looked down at the floor. "I know it's the same day as the dance, but would you want to come and be the cameraperson? We'd get back in time."

"Sure," Nick said. "I need to help the decorating

committee with the lights, but I'm not in charge of it. Let me ask my mom."

It would be another field trip for me and Nick! The first time was New York City. That was back when I was feeling definitely less comfortable around him. I never would have had the nerve to ask him to go somewhere before. Now that we were going to the dance together, I felt so much more casual and cool around him!

"Payton?" Nick asked.

"We can get a couple of people to work on it with us," I said. "Maybe Lakiya as a sound person and—"

"Payton—" Nick interrupted me.

"Or if you don't want Lakiya, you can choose someone else," I said hastily. "Maybe Willa?"

"Payton! Is that your late bus?" Nick asked, pointing to a bus that was closing its doors.

Ack! Yes! Yes, it was!

"Why, yes," I said, casual and cool-like. "I'll talk to you later."

The bus started pulling away.

"Oh no!" I yelped. So much for casual and cool. I ran down the sidewalk toward my bus.

"Hey! Wait!" I yelled. "Waiiiit!"

My heavy tote bag banged against my leg as I ran

awkwardly toward the bus. I could see people's faces as they laughed and pointed at me. And then, thankfully, the bus slowed down and came to a stop. The doors whooshed open, and I jumped on board.

"You're lucky I waited," the bus driver growled at me. "If it weren't for your sister driving me crazy . . ."

Emma sat in the seat behind the driver, looking smug. I slid into the seat next to her, breathing hard.

"I merely informed him that official district policy was that if a student is in sight trying to reach the bus, all efforts to wait for the student should be taken," Emma said.

"I didn't see her," the driver said.

"Emma, shush, you're embarrassing," I whispered.

"Well, I saw her, so she was in sight," Emma said to the driver loudly. Then she turned to me. "*I'm* embarrassing? Shall I do an imitation of you running to the bus? The bus that would have left without you had it not been for your loving twin?"

"Ergh." I sank in my seat. "I meant to say, 'Thank you, Emma.'"

"That's better," Emma said.

Fourteen

THE NEXT DAY, BEFORE SCHOOL

"Welcome to the team of our first *On the Scene* VOGS cast!" Mrs. Burkle clasped her hands joyfully. "That's what I'll be calling our traveling broadcasts: *On the Scene with VOGS!*"

We were sitting in the VOGS room. Mrs. Burkle had called Payton and me into a meeting before school started. I yawned. It was too early for Mrs. Burkle's enthusiasm.

"Hooray!" Payton was wide awake and full of excitement.

"Emma, although you are not a member of VOGS, you will be a special correspondent!" Mrs. Burkle sang out. "When we're at Multipalooza, you'll be coreporting with your twin sister."

"I will?" That woke me up.

"She will?" Payton said at the same time. I looked over at Payton. I could see her face fall with disappointment. I knew that she was hoping this was her show, her chance to shine on VOGS. I opened my mouth to stick up for her, but Mrs. Burkle cut me off.

"And here's the rest of the Multipalooza team!" she announced.

And in walked the triplets. Dexter. Oliver. And Asher. They were dressed in matching gray shirts, black jeans, and gray sneakers.

"Why are they here?" Payton whispered to me.

"My five correspondents for Multipalooza! Behind the scenes, part of the scenes," Mrs. Burkle said. "Identicals make great television!"

Payton slumped.

I watched as they each took a chair. I scanned them for differences. Even with my keen eye, I couldn't find any. No extra freckles, no hair that was springier, no eyebrows that were thicker. They were seriously identical.

As much as it was weird for people to do that to me and Payton (yes, her nose is bigger), I really wanted to identify which triplet was which. As a twin, I knew how I felt when people just lumped me in with my sister as "one of the twins" and didn't bother to figure out who was who.

Plus, for some reason I felt like they were being sneaky.

"Just so I don't mix you guys up and offend you," I said, "which of you is which?"

"We're DexterOliverAsher," one of them said, waving vaguely.

I was right. They didn't want us to know which was which. Fine, two—or four—could play that game. I would call them all Triplet.

"Mrs. Burkle, we have some ideas for Multipalooza segments. Since our aunt is on the board, we can get all the VIP behind-the-scenes access that other people can't."

They looked pointedly at Payton.

I knew it. They *were* being sneaky. I didn't know why, but I needed to find out.

"Why don't you all work together and make a list of your ideas? Then you can divide them up," Mrs. Burkle said.

I spoke quickly.

"Since this was Payton's idea, why doesn't she start?" I said, and smiled at Payton.

"Um," Payton said, looking panicked.

"Nothing? Well, here's what we need to do," a triplet jumped in. "We'll start the first segment, introduce our aunt, and then show everyone around."

"Since our aunt is on the board, we know the history of the festival, who the important people are, and where to go," a triplet said.

"I think that clinches it," Triplet #3 said, and nodded. "Plus, there's three of us. On-screen together, what could be better to introduce a festival for multiples? So, we'll start with—"

"No," I said firmly. "Payton will introduce the first segment. Payton, how do you want to start it?"

"RRfbflt," Payton stammered. "I can skkrbltff."

The triplets snickered in unison.

Oh no. Payton was choking under the pressure! Like I had once choked under the pressure of my first spelling bee (age three at the Precocious Pre-K Bee). I needed to help her save face.

"Brilliant," I told her. "Just brilliant."

The triplets, Mrs. Burkle, and Payton all swiveled their heads and looked at me, confused.

"Krrrzikni mlinokoff," I said. "Rflbt."

"*What* are you talking about?" a triplet said.

"Oh, sorry," I smiled. "Payton and I are talking in our secret twin language. We didn't mean to leave you out, right, Payton?"

I gave her a look. Hopefully she could understand that look meant, work with me.

"Right?" Payton said weakly.

"What Payton was suggesting was that she introduce the scene with myths about multiples, and then we can all do news stories to dispel them. Right, Payton?" I said.

Like the myth of triplet ESP, I was thinking.

"Right!" Payton said more confidently. "Pflmpt."

"You two have a secret twin language?" Mrs. Burkle clasped her hands. "I've always found that so fascinating when twins have their own language. Did you speak it as babies?"

Okay, maybe we weren't speaking a secret twin language now. But one of the common twin questions was "Do you have your own language?" And actually, Payton and I used to.

My mom has us on video talking to each other and making no sense at all—except to each other. I have to admit, we were quite adorable. Especially me. I was particularly verbal.

"We had a secret language too," one of the triplets said, butting in. "Back when we were *babies*."

"Well, there we go!" Mrs. Burkle said so loudly we all jumped. "Your twins segment will be interviewing twins about those questions we all have."

"Yes!" Payton finally got her voice. "Emma and I made a list of our Top Ten Questions People Ask Twins once."

"Divide the list between you, and there's a segment for the show," Mrs. Burkle said. "Payton can introduce it since it was her idea."

Bzzzt. The bell rang. It was time for the school day to start.

I walked out into the hallway and waited for Payton to join me.

"Ta-da!" I said to her. "Now you've regained control of your VOGS cast!"

The triplets came out into the hallway.

"Skkkblfffle," one of them said to us, and they all laughed.

"Kerblooey, Emma," another one said. "Poopy-doopy doodles."

"If you're trying to embarrass us, it's not working," I said, hoping they wouldn't notice Payton blushing in embarrassment. "You're just irritated because *we* are going to rule the VOGS cast."

The bell to start school went off, and I grinned as the triplets walked away.

"We did it," I told Payton as we walked toward our lockers. "We're a good team!"

"Bluh," she said.

"What? We totally dominated those triplets," I said.

"We're supposed to be a team," she said. "Everyone on VOGS works together. It's not one of your competitions."

"Well, those triplets made it one," I said. "Did you see how they were trying to take it over from you?"

I looked at her sternly.

"This is like Ashlynn making you a fashion slave or Sydney trying to boss you around," I said. "You need to stand up for yourself. Go, Payton! Go, Twins!"

"Go, Geckos!" someone walking by called out.

"Go, Geckos!" I responded, punching the air.

"Thanks," Payton said. "You're right. This is my chance to show Mrs. Burkle and everyone my mad reporting skills."

"And if you need help," I said, "I'll be there."

"Thanks for the pep talk," Payton said. "Go, Team

Mills!" She punched the air, like I usually do.

"Go, Team Mills!" I agreed. We both laughed. I was glad my pep talk worked. There were times to cooperate, and there were times to compete.

Multipalooza would be . . . both.

Fifteen

EARLY MULTIPALOOZA MORNING

Emma and I were doing something we hadn't done since our mother made us do it when we were four.

We dressed alike. Exactly alike. On purpose.

I had never felt more identical . . . and closer to my twin. Even though we were dressed the same for the Multipalooza festival, I felt like we were bonding, having a moment of closeness. I looked at Emma. Was she feeling it too?

"This is . . ." Emma paused. "Weird. I feel like we're clones, a science experiment gone wrong."

Nope. Identical outfits don't make for identical thinking.

❀ 111 ❀

"I thought we were kind of cute," I said.

"Oh," Emma said. "Sorry. That too."

"I think you both look great," my dad said from the front seat of the car. Our car pulled in to the school parking lot, where we were going to meet up with everyone going to Multipalooza.

I had wanted to be the best on camera we could be and had researched what real news reporters wore. No white (it glows and I didn't want us to be ghost twins), no patterns (they can look like they're moving), and no shiny jewelry (it can reflect light).

The websites had recommended blues, purples, or greens. I also noticed a lot of news reporters wearing blazers. So at the last minute I had begged Mom to take us shopping and forced Emma to match me. We were both wearing:

* Deep blue blazer
* Pale green tank
* Skinny black pants
* Small gold earrings
* Black flats

"We *do* look professional," Emma said. "You did well. It will add credibility to our reporting, and later, when I interview subjects for my science fair project."

This was the busiest day of my entire life! First, our road trip to Multipalooza! Being a VOGS reporter! Assisting Emma with her science fair project! Then tonight was the Autumn Dance!

Eek! Yayyy! Eeeekkk! Could I handle so much excitement and nervousness? The more I thought about it, the more I realized that the answer might be no.

My heart was racing, my skin was clammy, and I felt dizzy.

"I'm freaking out," I whispered to Emma. "Being on VOGS at Multipalooza *and* the dance tonight. I think it's too much for me."

"Deep breaths," advised Emma. "In through the nose, out through the mouth."

I breathed as Emma gave me more advice.

"I've been in this situation many times," she said. "Remember when I had the regional spelling bee, went to Dad's office picnic, and got stung by a bee all in one day?"

I nodded. She was making me feel better. First, by being nice. And second, at least I didn't have to be doing all these things with a swollen, bee-stung nose.

"You girls have a fun time," my dad said. "Break a leg for your video show!"

"Thanks," we said.

We said good-bye to Dad and walked toward the group of people in the parking lot. I headed over to where Nick was standing with some of the video equipment.

"Hey," Nick said. "You look nice."

"Thanks!" I said. "I'm kind of nervous for the VOGS."

"You shouldn't be," Nick said. "You do a great job. Plus, it's not live, so we can always edit it. This will be a cool show."

Suddenly loud guitar music started playing. Everyone turned to see where it was coming from.

"It's the triplets," Emma said, nudging me. The triplets were wearing identical gray hats, black T-shirts, checkered short-sleeved shirts, and black jeans. And making an entrance, as they strutted up toward the parking lot. One of them was strumming his guitar.

"Eeee! It's the SuperTwins!" Girls came after them, screaming. Well, two girls anyway.

Sydney? Cashmere?

"What are they doing here?" Emma whispered to me.

I looked closer. Sydney was wearing a white T-shirt that had what looked like ironed-on letters: SUPERTWINS.

"Yay, SuperTwins!" Cashmere squealed. She held up a yellow poster board covered in glitter:

Supertwins
The next big SUPERgroup!

"Looks like the triplets have SuperFans," Nick said.

"SuperGroupies." Emma nodded.

"Do you think they're just here to wave them goodbye, or do you think they're coming with us?" I asked, hoping for the first.

Sydney and Cashmere at Multipalooza? Bleh.

"Hi, everyone!" Sydney said as they both came up to us. "Surprised to see me?"

"Well, you're not a multiple, you're not in VOGS, so—yes," Emma said.

"We're officially helping out the SuperTwins," Sydney said. "They invited us!"

"Just like Sydney invited the triplets to the dance with her," Cashmere added brightly. "But they said no!"

"Because they'd be at the festival," Sydney said quickly. "That's why."

"Well, we'll be at the festival *and* the dance, so why can't they?" Cashmere shrugged.

Sydney's face crumpled, and as she gripped the poster board, I felt a little sorry for her.

"Well, their mom and aunt are running the festival, so they probably need to get back late," I offered. "Maybe they won't have time to pick up dates and everything. Lots of people are going without dates, anyway."

"Well, now I'm going with Reilly instead," Sydney said, perking up. "He's an *eighth grader* and a great dancer. I bet Ox is a great dancer. You should be so excited to dance with him!"

I was expecting some gratitude, but I should have known better. Sydney knew Emma couldn't dance—and wouldn't in public. Fortunately, Emma couldn't be tortured on this one.

"Sure," Emma said to her.

"I'll dance with him if you don't," Sydney said.

Emma clutched my arm. I sent her twin telepathic messages:

—*Don't let Sydney get to you! We have enough to worry about.*

—*It's probably not true, anyway!*

—*And if it is, well . . . make sure everyone knows it's you dancing and not me!*

"Aren't you on the dance committee?" Nick stepped

in smoothly. "Shouldn't you be back there setting up or something?"

"A good leader delegates," Sydney said. "I've got my committee hard at work."

That would include Quinn and Tess, hard at work. I'd texted Tess earlier, and she told me they were already at the gym decorating and setting up for tonight.

"I knew the SuperTwins would need me," Sydney said. "Nick, have you met them?"

"I met Asher," he said. "He's in my French class, but I haven't met his brothers."

"Hey!" Sydney suddenly yelled. "SuperTwins! Get over here!"

I wasn't surprised when the triplets hustled over.

"Boys. This is Nick. If you haven't met him, he's in charge of the VOGS cast today," she said. "He'll film you at your most flattering, right, Nick?"

"I guess you could put it that way." Nick grinned. "So, you psyched for your performance today?"

"Yep," two of the triplets said in unison. The third one said it a split second later. "Yep."

"We're going to rock Multipalooza," one said. "Get it all on video. It'll be worth something."

"Soon," a triplet added.

"I can't wait to see you play," Sydney cooed. "I bet you're amazing."

"Oh yeah, that reminds me," one of the triplets said, and turned to Sydney. "Some of our equipment needs to be loaded into your car. So you can go take care of that."

"What?" Sydney asked him.

"The amps, the mike," a triplet said. "You can load it into the car you're traveling in."

"I'm a *groupie*, not a roadie," Sydney said. "Yeesh. I'm not lifting anything."

"Do it yourself," Emma said.

"We're the talent. We can't risk injury," a triplet said, and held up his hands.

"Maybe that muscley dude will do it," a triplet said, pointing to someone.

I saw Emma's eyes light up and turned to look. Yup. Ox was walking toward us.

"He *is* muscley," Emma agreed, smiling.

"Hi," he said to everyone. Then he turned to Emma. "Hey."

"Ox, you're not on VOGS," Sydney said. "Why are you here?"

"He's here to help with equipment and things," Emma told her.

"Oh, good, we need a roadie," one of the triplets said.

"We need the amp and the mike brought over," another said. "And fast."

Ox raised an eyebrow at them.

"He's here to help with the VOGS equipment," Emma said. "You have Sydney and Cashmere to help you out."

"I'll do it!" Cashmere said brightly. "My brother always tells me that my arm muscles are stronger than my brain muscles!"

She flexed her arms.

Nobody even touched that one.

"People!" Mrs. Burkle said, heading our way. "People of our first remote VOGS ever. Huddle!" We all gathered around her. "Thank you, chaperones and drivers. There will be three vehicles in the caravan. Students, report to your assigned vehicle as follows:

"Car Number One: Dexter, Oliver, Asher, in your mother's car.

"Car Number Two: Sydney, Cashmere, and Lakiya. You'll be in my car."

That was one car I was glad I was not in.

"In Car Number Three: Emma, Payton, Ox, Nick . . ."

Ooh! Ooh! Also eek and yay! It was like a double date in our car. Maybe it would be a big SUV with three rows of seats. I could sit with Nick in the back, Emma and Ox in front of us. Nick and I could hold hands. It would be romantic.

Emma and I smiled.

". . . and . . ." Mrs. Burkle kept talking. Wait, *and*? And who?

"Mason Case-Babbitt and Jason Case-Babbitt. You'll all be in with Coach Babbitt and Counselor Case."

Emma and I stopped smiling.

A silver minivan pulled up in front of us. The door rolled open to reveal Mason and Jason sitting inside.

"Get in!" Jason called out. "We're road trippin'!"

"Woot! Our car rocks!" Mason hooted.

"And smells!" Jason said, wrinkling his nose. "Ew, what stinks?"

"I took my shoes off to get comfortable." Mason stuck his sock in the air and wiggled his foot around.

Emma and I looked at each other and simultaneously sighed. So much for the double date.

"I call you sit in the backseat with Mason and Jason," I whispered to Emma.

"I call we put Mason and Jason in the trunk," Emma whispered back.

Sixteen

ON THE WAY TO MULTIPALOOZA

"I want to sit next to Emma! We can talk about math!" Jason said, leaning forward from the backseat. He slid over in his seat and patted it.

"I'll sit next to Payton," Mason said from the middle seat. "She won't talk about math with me! Wait, I want to sit next to Ox, too. Ox, did you see the game last night?"

"Good, because I want to sit next to Nick," Jason said. "Nick, can we shoot a movie in the car?"

"Don't you boys want to sit together?" Payton asked them, trying to sound cheerful.

"We can't," Jason said. "We have to sit in these

stupid seats with these stupid kid seat belts. Like we're babies."

Ah, they were sitting in booster-style seats in each row.

"Mom keeps us separated as far as possible in the car," Mason said.

"Mason has to sit closer to Mom so she can make sure he doesn't get in trouble," Jason said.

"No punching, kicking, or poking," Mason sighed.

"Well, if I sit next to one of you guys, that rule has be enforced," Ox said. "I don't want to get hurt."

I smiled at Ox. One of the best things about Ox was that he looked so tough, but he was really sweet.

"I won't! I won't hurt you," Mason said, banging on the seat next to him. "Sit here!"

"Looks like you're sitting there," I told Ox. I was about to slide into the middle seat when Jason yelled from the backseat, "No, Emma! You're back here with me so we can do math equations! Pleeeease?"

Well. It was hard to say no to math equations. Plus, sitting next to Ox for a whole hour in the car would be distracting. Today was going to be intense, helping my sister with the VOGS cast and being on sensory overload with multiples. Not to mention trying not to think about tonight's dance.

I got in on one side of Jason, and Nick got in on the other. Payton slid into the seat in front of me on one side of Mason, Ox into the other.

"Everyone buckled?" Coach Babbitt started the car. Our car inched out and got into a line with the triplets' car and Mrs. Burkle's van. And we were off!

Off to Multipalooza!

"Let us know if you need anything," Counselor Case said.

"I have to go to the bathroom," Jason said.

"Don't even start," Coach Babbitt told him. "You just went."

He turned on the radio.

"It's Seventies Flashback Saturday here at WTLY," the announcer said.

"Oh man, not the old-people station," Mason groaned.

"Don't defame my music," Counselor Case said. "Oh, one of my childhood favorites!"

She turned the radio up louder.

"Agh! What is that horrible noise?" Jason yelped, holding his ears.

"Noise?!" Counselor Case gasped. "It's a song from one of my favorite movies, *Grease*."

"You *don't* want to insult your mother's favorite

movie," Coach Babbitt warned. "I learned that the hard way."

"I know all the words to this song," Counselor Case said cheerfully. Then she started singing along.

"Maaaa, stop. You're so embarrassing," Mason groaned.

"*I'm* embarrassing you for a change?" Counselor Case said. "Finally! Hey, did you know there are hand motions to this song? It's called the hand jive!"

She started doing a clapping-and-waving-her-hands-in-the-air thing.

"Payton and Nick, you may want to learn the hand jive," Counselor said. "I wouldn't be surprised if your drama club performs *Grease* someday. Bertha Burkle is a fan."

"MA! You're torturing us." Mason shrunk down in his seat.

"Oh, *you've* never 'tortured anyone,' right, Mason?" I teased him. "It looks too complicated for you guys anyway."

"It's not too complicated for us!" Jason protested. "Mom, show us."

"I'll learn it, too. In case I ever audition for *Grease*," Payton said, leaning forward.

"I dare everyone in the car to try it," Coach Babbitt said.

"Oh, sure, that's because *you're* driving, so you can't," Ox pointed out.

Counselor Case patted her hands on her lap twice, clapped twice, and did some more hand movements that ended in her doing thumbs-up over her shoulders. Then she repeated it faster.

Everyone tried to follow, clapping and patting and thumbs-upping.

"Wow, Emma, you're good!" Counselor Case said.

Me? Doing well at a form of dance?

"It's simply a matter of two moves to a four-four beat," I said modestly. "Ox, you're doing very well yourself."

"Thanks," he said. "I try."

The song ended, and everyone laughed.

"They did the hand jive at the school dance in *Grease*," Counselor Case said. "It was so romantic with Danny and Sandy until someone came along and stole Danny from Sandy on the dance floor—"

"Hey, Mom," Jason interrupted. "Isn't that another one of your favorite songs on?"

"No, but it's one of mine," Coach said. "I'm cranking

this up and can't hear you back there. Kick my seat if someone bleeds."

"Good save, Jason," Mason nodded. "Get the parents out of our business."

"Speaking of kicking," Jason said. "Ox and Nick, I hope you guys don't get kicked out today. You're not even twins, and you're trying to get into a twins festival."

"What do you mean?" Ox asked. "Nick and I are twins."

Ox turned around and gave me a quick wink.

"You are?" Mason asked. "Who are your twins?"

"Each other," Ox said. "Fraternal, obviously."

"Yeah, I'm older," Nick said, playing along. "Six minutes."

"No WAY!" Mason said. "I didn't know that. You guys look so different."

"You think?" Ox asked. "Sometimes people get us mixed up. They think I'm Nick."

"They call me Ox," Nick agreed. "Sometimes they just call us Oxnick, if they don't know who is who."

Bzzzzrpt!

I had a text from Payton.

lol

"Wait a minute, people can't mix you guys up. You

look different," Jason said suspiciously. "Plus you have different last names and live in different houses."

Payton started to crack up first, then we all started laughing.

"You aren't twins," Mason finally caught on. "You're tricking us."

"Had you going," Nick said. "But when I was a kid, I wished I was a twin."

"You did?" Payton asked him.

"Yeah, I had an imaginary twin," Nick said. "His name was Captain Hero."

Now all of us, especially the twins, laughed.

"You really want to laugh at me? Or should I bring up *your* nicknames from that age, Emma and Payton?" Nick said.

"I'm not laughing." I put on a straight face, and Payton quickly did the same.

"What were your nicknames? Tell us! Tell us!" Mason and Jason begged.

"No way," I said.

"I'll tell you Jason's nickname," Mason offered.

"Hey!" Jason protested. "Then I'll tell them about *your* imaginary friends. Mason made us into quadruplets. The other two were action figures."

"They were cool dudes," Mason said, offended. "Grayson and Fason."

"Fason?" I tried not to laugh.

"Fake Mason," Mason said.

"Or Fake Jason," Jason said.

"You were just making fun of him," Mason said. "So he obviously was *not* Fake Jason. Actually, Fason didn't like you."

"He didn't? What did I do?" Jason said. He actually sounded upset.

"Guys!" I said. "Guys! We're not arguing about imaginary friends."

"I was never mean to Fason," Jason continued. "But I'll be mean to you."

"Then I'll tell your nickname—" Mason threatened.

I looked to see if their parents were noticing, but they were too busy singing along to the oldies.

"Twin fight," Payton said. We knew how those went.

"Guys, enough," I said. "Look, stop fighting and I'll tell you Payton's and my nicknames for each other when we were little."

Ox and Nick both grinned. They already knew them, unfortunately, from a time Payton and I overshared.

I sighed and told them.

"BWAHAHAHAHAHAHA" Mason and Jason immediately forgot about their fighting. "Who was who?"

"I was MeeMa," I said. "Payton was PeePa."

Mason and Jason were laughing so hard, we all started cracking up.

Suddenly my phone made an alert noise.

"Whose phone is that?" Jason asked. "Is it PeePee's?"

"PeePA." Payton sighed. "Why, oh why, didn't I give Emma a worse name?"

"Poopy," Mason said cracking himself up. "You could be PeePee and Poopy."

"We've heard that one before," Payton grumbled.

"Uh-oh," I said, checking my texts. "My traffic app went off. Traffic is stopped here, you may want to take an alternate route off the next exit, exit fourteen, instead."

"Well, that's certainly helpful," Counselor Case said. "We have to let the other cars know. Do you have their numbers?"

"I have Sydney's and—oh wait, I have one of the triplets' numbers," I said.

"You do?" Payton asked.

"Their mother had me give it to them at the Chinese

restaurant when we met them," I reminded her. "It's under Triplet."

"Can I text them? Can I? Can I?" Mason asked. "I never get to text, and I'm really good at typing from all my hours on Club Walrus."

"Okay," I handed Mason my cell. "Text them that we're pulling over at the next rest area."

"Thank you, Emma," Counselor Case said.

"Hey, Ox! Emma! Press your noses up to the window," Mason suddenly said. "I can't reach!"

"And we're doing that because . . . ?" Nick asked.

"Hurry!" Mason said. "I'll explain in a minute. Trust me!"

"Trust *you*?" Jason said.

But Ox just grinned and squashed his face against the window.

"Yeeesss!" Mason said. "C'mon, Emma!"

I wasn't sure I wanted to know why I had to do this. But I squashed my nose against the window too.

Suddenly, the triplets' SUV pulled alongside us again, and I could see the triplets' faces. They were all laughing.

"Mason! The triplets' car is there, and they're all laughing at us!" I said. Argh. Maybe they'd think I was Payton.

"Oh, sorry," Mason said, not sounding sorry at all. Hmmm.

"Wait, what are they doing over there?" Payton asked. I looked and saw that the triplets' faces were no longer laughing. Instead they were making some weird faces at us.

"Monkey faces," Mason said. "Chimpanzees, to be precise."

"Mason, what's going on?" Payton asked.

"Just a little friendly innocent wager," Mason said innocently. "Okay, I dared the triplets to act like monkeys. They said they would if we would act like pigs. Oh wait a sec—"

Bzzzzrpt!

My cell phone went off. I had a text.

"Mason? My cell phone?" I asked him, holding my hand over the seat.

"Just a second," he said. "Hey! They say their monkey faces beat our pig faces. You didn't squish your noses up enough."

"Wait, who says what?" I asked him. "You were just supposed to be texting them about the gas station."

"Uh—" Mason said.

"Payton, get that cell."

With a little help from Ox, Payton wrestled the cell phone away from Mason and handed it to me over the seat. I read out loud:

"Emma: *Take next exit: 14. we know what were doing.*

"Sydney Star: *k.*"

I scrolled to the next one.

"Emma: *Take next exit: 14. we know what were doing.*

"Emma: *Dare u to make munky faces at us!*

"Supertwin 1: *only if u make pig faces first.*

"Emma: *k.*

"SUPERTWIN 1: *our monkey faces ruled. We win u LOSE.*

"They think *I* texted them that? You didn't say it was you?" I sputtered. "They think I spelled 'monkey' wrong?"

"Move on," Mason said. "The real problem is they think they were better than us."

Bzzzzrpt!

A picture text came up. It was the triplets, all holding up "L for Loser" fingers.

I hadn't known we were in competition. But now that I did, I texted something back.

Emma: *Double-dare?*

Supertwin 1: *Bring it. Make ur ugliest faces.*

"We have been double-dared," I announced. "Get ready! When their car pulls up again, make your ugliest faces."

"They're pulling up," Nick said. We all leaned toward the window. The SUV pulled alongside again.

"One, two, three, go!" Ox called out.

Everyone made their ugliest faces. We could see the triplets pointing and laughing.

Bzzzzrpt!

A picture text came up that was cc'd to Sydney too. I could see all of us making ugly faces through the window.

Supertwin 1: caption: *Twins try to beat Triplets? Fail!*

Sydney Star: *Yearbook photo!!*

"Rude!" I said as I passed the phone around so everyone could see.

"You and Payton are making the same exact face," Nick pointed out. We had both pulled our mouths wide and crossed our eyes.

"All right, we have to double-dare them back," I said. "Ideas?"

Mason had the best idea. I texted the other car what to do. We all watched out the side window as the triplets' faces appeared in the window. But before they could do their challenge, the car lines merged. The triplets' car had to pull in front of us.

"Ha! They missed their chance," I said. "We win."

I texted them: *WE WIN*.

Supertwin 1: *Not yet! Wait for it . . .*

We didn't have to wait long.

"What in heaven's name are they doing?" Counselor Case said, and gasped.

The triplets were looking out the back window. They made kissy faces. Then they blew kisses at us.

"Are the new students sending us kisses?" Counselor Case asked, sounding confused.

"It looks like they are," Ox said with a straight face.

"Do they know who they are sending kisses to?" Counselor Case asked.

"Uh-oh," Payton and I said at the same time.

"So they don't realize they're blowing kisses at their guidance counselor and coach?" Coach Babbitt confirmed.

We all burst out laughing and told them what was going on.

"It was Mason's idea but my fault," I said. "I couldn't resist. It was a competition. I thought they would look out the side window at *us*, not you."

"Perhaps you shouldn't tell them," Counselor Case. "We don't want to embarrass them."

"Too late," Mason said, holding up my phone. "I already texted them."

"Yes, I just realized that," Counselor Case said.

I peered out the front window and saw a look of horror pass over the triplets' faces. Then they turned around, and their faces disappeared.

"I think they're hiding," Ox said. "Wise move."

"Mason, give me back my phone," I said. "You've already caused enough crazy."

I read what he texted.

Emma: *LOL U just blew kisses at guidance counselor and the coach.*

"Um, you didn't make it clear he was the *Mathletes* coach?" I asked.

"Mathletes coach, football coach." Mason shrugged. "Practically the same thing. Right, Dad?"

"Mathematics is nothing to be ashamed of," Coach Babbitt said. "I hold my head high. Dignified. Leader-like. AGH! What the heck was that?"

"Oops," Mason said. "Sorry! My bubble gum got away from me. I spit instead of blew."

Ew. Gross. I hoped we were almost there.

"Okay, boys. Settle down," Coach Babbitt said, wiping the back of his neck with a tissue.

Then Counselor Case said, "Oh, look out your window!"

I looked out the window and saw a huge sign:

Multipalooza!
1 mile ahead!

We *were* almost there!

Payton

Seventeen

AT MULTIPALOOZA!

Squee! Multiple squee! We were at Multipalooza!

We followed Counselor Case into the fairgrounds.

"So everyone who is a twin already has a ticket," Coach Babbitt said, handing us our tickets. "Emma, Payton, can you take our boys to wait over by the entrance where we can see you while I bring the nontwins to the sign-in booth? We'll pick up your tickets."

"Mason and Jason, I got you disposable cameras for the day," Counselor Case said.

"Cool!" Mason and Jason took them.

The twins immediately started taking funny pictures

of each other. And that gave me a minute to look into the festival.

Wow.

Everywhere I looked, there were identicals. Adults, teenagers, kids. Two, three, four, dressed like each other, looking like each other . . .

Double wow.

Of course, I was an identical twin. And I know we're fun to notice. When Emma and I were little, people would say, "Oh! Identical twins!" And even now, people do double takes or ask us what it's like.

Being here, surrounded by identicals, I had a feeling of . . . camaraderie. These thousands of people walking around Multipalooza would understand the kinds of things Emma and I went through. The fun and the annoyance of people mixing us up, comparing us, commenting on us.

These were *our* people! Emma walked up next to me and was looking out over the crowd. I bet she was thinking the exact same thing!

"What are you thinking?" I asked her.

"I'm thinking if the incidence of identical twins in this country is four per thousand, then the percentage of twins here is—"

"Emma," I said. "For one moment stop thinking about percentages. Just look at all of the identicals! Isn't this amazing? It's like we're surrounded by people like us."

"You're right," Emma said.

"It seems so special," I said. "Not better than everyone else, but just special."

"Wrong! We are special *and* better than everyone else," someone said. "We're the . . . SuperTwins!"

The triplets had arrived. And apparently had excellent hearing.

"We're here," one posed. "Check out all of our future fans. Little do they know, they're about to hear greatness today."

"You guys have triple-sized egos," Emma said.

"We're stars," a triplet said, and shrugged.

"That's why we're going to star in your Frogscast," a triplet added.

"Who said you're *starring* in the VOGS cast?" I said. "There's plenty to film. Look around!"

"Well, it's a school show. We assume you're going to focus on the biggest deal that has ever hit our middle school—the SuperTwins!"

The triplets posed.

Hmmm. They were kinda right. But I didn't want to tell them that.

Mason and Jason came over to us.

"Ha-ha! You guys blew kisses at our parents!" Mason said. "That was hilarious!"

"Yeah, well, we didn't know who they were," one triplet said. All three turned bright red.

"That means we win the double-dare! You lose!" Jason said.

"That doesn't mean we lose," a triplet protested. "We did our challenges: monkey faces and kisses."

"And we did ours," Emma said.

"So we're tied," Payton said. "A good way to end."

"What?" Emma, Jason, and two of the triplets looked at me.

"You can't end a competition with a tie," Emma said. "We need a tiebreaker for the ride home."

"Why does it have to be the ride home?" a triplet said. "Why not now?"

"Yeah! Dare us now!" Jason challenged.

"We can take you," Mason said. "Challenge us at any of the Multipalooza competitions. Like . . ."

Jason held up what looked like a Multipalooza brochure.

"We challenge you to a duel! Which will it be—Multipalooza Chairs? Or—Multipalooza Sack Races?"

"Guys, you can't challenge us to those," a triplet said.

"What?" Mason put his arm around his brother's shoulder. "You think just because there's three of you that you're better than two?"

"No, because you're in the *younger* division," a triplet said. "We'd be in the twelve-to-fourteens."

"Oh," Jason said, looking disappointed. "Well, then, Emma and Payton can challenge you!"

Um, what?

"That's—" I started to say "That's not a good idea" when Emma jumped in.

"That's a great idea," Emma said.

"Dare you," Mason said.

"Double-dare you," a triplet added. "No, wait, triple-dare you."

"So we'd compete in Multipalooza events against you guys?" I asked.

"Yes!" Emma said.

"What?!" I turned to her. "Not yes? NO! The answer is NO!"

"Payton, they triple-dared us," Emma said.

Oh, yeesh. Emma could not turn down a competition. Emma looked at me. "Okay?"

"Uh, we're pretty busy today," I said. "I have to film VOGS."

"Genius! We can film the competition on VOGS!" Jason clapped.

"Gak!" I sputtered. This was getting worse and worse!

"That's not a bad idea," Emma said.

That's it. Emma was losing her mind.

"Emma, I need to talk to you *privately*," I hissed.

I pulled her off to the side.

"A competition against the triplets filmed on VOGS?" I whisper-shrieked. "How could that possibly be a good idea? Just because you need to compete, don't drag me into it."

"I admit, I get carried away when challenged with a competition," Emma agreed. "But it has benefits for both of us."

Benefits? Being humiliated on VOGS in front of the entire school? We'd already done that! When we'd done our first Twin Switch and then been busted on VOGS and gotten in a fight on VOGS!

"Think about this objectively for a minute," Emma said. "You wanted to win a spot as a VOGS anchor, right? So think about this: What does Mrs. Burkle want? An exciting VOGS cast that people will watch, so the principal will give her more budget and airtime."

"How do you know these things?" I asked.

"Mrs. Burkle had me proofread her annual performance review when I finished my English test," Emma said, and shrugged.

"So focus on your goal: making a splash on VOGS," she continued. "With this competition, you'll be a traveling reporter who actually is part of the action. Instead of just standing and interviewing people we don't know."

It would be something students would want to watch, I had to admit. But . . .

"But it could be embarrassing," I said.

"But FUN embarrassing," Emma said.

I opened my mouth to protest and then shut it. Since when did Emma think about FUN? I looked at her suspiciously. Whoa, I think Emma actually meant it. Emma was convincing *me* to have fun?

"Okay," I said weakly. Then louder. "Let's do it."

I marched back over to the triplets.

"We officially accept your challenge," I said. "Multipalooza MILLS TWINS Versus Whatever Your Last Name Is TRIPLETS!"

"YEEESSS!" Mason and Jason hooted and pumped their fists.

Well, okay. Maybe we could have some fun with this.

"Twins Versus Triplets!" Emma pumped her fist and did an awkward little hoot. "Woot, woot!"

And the "fun" embarrassment had begun.

"We need to set some guidelines," Emma said. "The competitions have to be fair since obviously you have three and we have two . . ."

"You two can take their three!" Mason cheered. "Twins rule, Triplets drool!"

"Triplets rule, Twins will be schooled!" a triplet responded.

"Yeah! SuperTwins rock!" New voices cheered from behind us. Sydney and Cashmere were bopping up, holding their SuperTwins posters.

"Emma and Payton are going to take down your SuperTwins!" Mason yelled.

"You're going to perform in a band too?" Cashmere asked us.

"Yeesh, no," I said. Emma and I couldn't sing. That would be beyond embarrassing, and not the "fun" kind.

"Hey, Mrs. Burkle said she's almost done making

the VOGS arrangements," Ox said as he walked up with Nick and the tech crew.

"What'd we miss?" Nick asked us.

MULTIPALOOZA TWINS VERSUS TRIPLETS DOUBLE-TRIPLE CHALLENGE!

It was ON!

Eighteen

MULTIPALOOZA MERCHANDISING

"Twins are TWICE as NICE!"

"We're TWINspiring!"

We all stood at the merchandising stand, looking at the T-shirts for sale.

"Oh, that one is perfect!" I pointed at a bright green shirt with glittery silver foil letters that said "Twins are TWO-riffic!" with two pink lipstick kisses on it.

"Yes, that one is a definite," Payton agreed.

No, we hadn't lost our sense of fashion. We weren't picking out T-shirts for ourselves. We were checking out T-shirts we hoped the triplets would be wearing later today, on VOGS.

This was our bet: Whoever lost TWINS Versus TRIPLETS would have to wear T-shirts the other twins chose on VOGS. If they lost, we'd get to talk about why twins are better than triplets. I won't even mention the other outcome.

Of course, we'd be picking out "Twins are better"–themed shirts for the triplets to wear. I have to admit, I glanced over at the T-shirts in the triplets' section of the stand.

"Triplets are THREE TIMES the awesome!"

"Triple trouble!"

Some were really cute. Others were painful. I shuddered and hoped I didn't have to wear any of them.

"Heh!" Mason laughed and pointed at the stand. "That baby T-shirt says 'Parents of twins have double duty.' Doody! Heh!"

"Think we can force the triplets to wear those?" I grinned at Ox.

"Checking out what you're going to wear later?" The triplets came up behind us, followed by Sydney and Cashmere.

"Choosing *your* clothes," I said. "You can let the whole school know twins are better."

"What do you mean wear later? The whole school?"

Cashmere asked. "Wait, you're not wearing those T-shirts to the school dance, are you?"

"No!" Not only did Payton and I yell that in unison, but the triplets did too!

"The losers have to wear them on VOGS," Payton explained.

"Plus, we're not going to the dance," one of the triplets added.

"You are now," Sydney said. "I saw your mother at the sign-in area and convinced her to get you there, since it's your new school and you should participate. You'll just be a little late."

"What?" the triplets said in unison.

"Sydney's date has food poisoning," Cashmere explained. "So she needs a date. She chose you guys."

Well, this was an interesting development! I looked to see the triplets' reactions. I seemed to recall they already had turned her down once.

"All of us?" a triplet asked.

"Don't you think you should ask us first?" A triplet turned to her.

"Hmmm. Remember when you asked me to autograph the pictures of you to give away after your performance today? The five hundred photos?" Sydney asked, putting her hands on her hips. "And said you'd owe me one?"

"I didn't say that!" two of the triplets said.

"I did," one groaned.

Heh. Usually it was annoying to see Sydney win and get her way. This time, it was actually entertaining. Emma was grinning too. Hee hee hee.

"Time to pay up," Sydney said. "The SuperTwins are going to the Autumn Dance! And don't worry. I told my mom to pick out a corsage, so you don't have to worry about it. Pink and white."

"Yeah, that's what I'm worried about," the triplet next to me muttered. I was about to think of a good comeback when I noticed he was clutching his stomach. His face looked kind of greenish.

I recognized that look. It was a look I always tried to hide before sudden-death rounds in competitions. A combination of stage fright, competitive spirit, and possibly too much dairy. At least in my case. And the look of trying to hide it from everyone else so nobody would notice his nerves.

I'd been there. When he walked away, I wasn't surprised.

"Be right back," I said to Ox. I followed the triplet.

"Hey," I said. "You okay?"

"Me? Yeah, great," he said. "Ready to beat you twins. Yeah."

Then he clutched his stomach.

"There's a garbage can there," I pointed out. "If you need to throw up. Do you want me to get your mom?"

"Aughhh," he moaned. "No. Not yet. I just need a minute."

"And an antacid?" I pulled a little bottle of stomach tablets out of my backpack.

"Thanks," he said, taking one. "Wait, is this a trick? Are you trying to take me out of the competition?"

"Nah," I said. "I fight fair. If you can't participate, there is no competition. Plus, I don't want you vomiting on the playing fields. I can recognize the signs of nerves anywhere."

He ate an antacid tablet.

"Don't tell my brothers," he said. "They call me the 'wimpy triplet.' It's bad enough my mom calls me the 'sensitive triplet.'"

Aha, this would be Asher.

Asher's cell went off, and he pulled it out to read a text.

"Sydney says everyone has arrived, so get over there,"

Asher said. "I can't believe I'm going to the dance with that girl. She's going to boss us around."

"Well," I said carefully. "A lot of guys in school would be happy to go to the school dance with Sydney. She's in charge of the dance committee, so I'm sure you guys can rule the dance together."

"I think I'll just stay home sick all day," Asher said, clutching his stomach. "I can miss the dance and the performance."

"You don't want to perform?" I asked him.

"Nah," he said. "My brothers want to be rock stars. I get sick just thinking about being onstage later."

He turned a darker shade of green.

"Diagnosis: stage fright," I said. "What do you usually do to get over it before you perform?"

"I don't know. We've never performed before real people," he said.

"So those stories about the SuperTwins being a big group in your old town?"

"We played in our garage. Don't tell my brothers I told you that," he said. "The only reason we got this gig was because our aunt runs the event. We're going to make total fools of ourselves. I mean, we're okay on the guitars, but we really can't sing."

"You sang on VOGS," I said.

"The only three notes in the key we can pull off," he said miserably. "Anything higher or lower . . . It's painful. I think my brothers are tone-deaf. They really think they're good."

"Sorry," I said. "I know what it's like to feel compelled to do something you don't want to do because of twin pressure."

We had a moment of empathy between us.

"Usually when I am doing something humiliating, I just pretend I'm Dexter or Oliver," Asher said. "Then people think *they're* embarrassing."

We both laughed.

"But now we'll be onstage all together," he groaned. "I can't hide. This is going to be the worst day. Performing, then having to go to this dance . . ."

Suddenly, I saw the other two triplets coming up behind Asher. I knew he wouldn't want them to see him being upset—especially talking to me.

". . . Having to wear a–T-shirt about how it's better to be a twin on VOGS," I added loudly.

"Yeah and—wait, what?" Asher asked.

"Twins will win," I said, confidently and very loudly.

"Twins will LOSE!" the two triplets yelled back.

Asher looked startled and turned to see them.

"Yeah!" Asher stood up straight and took a deep breath. "SuperTwins will win!"

"Why are you hanging out at the trash can, Wimpy Twin?" one of the triplets said to Asher.

"He's *trash* talking," I said. Heh. That was pretty clever. "How is that wimpy? He thinks you guys can beat my sister and me? Ha!"

Out of the corner of my eye, Asher shot me a grateful look. I felt good about helping him feel better. But that was the last help he was going to get from me.

"Everyone's here, and the VOGS is set up," a triplet said. "It's time."

Nineteen

LIVE! FROM MULTIPALOOZA

"We're live from Multipalooza! A festival for twins, triplets, and multiple identicals! I'm Payton! And this is my—"

"Emma!" Emma said.

"Cut!" I said.

Nick put down the video camera.

I looked at Emma. "You're supposed to wait until I say 'my identical twin.' *Then* you say Emma."

"Sorry," Emma said. "I thought you were saying, 'And this is' and I was supposed to say my name."

"It did look like that," the girl who was backup for tech crew said. "Payton, you pointed at your sister, so it looked like she was supposed to—"

"Okay, okay," I said. "My bad. Maybe we should practice first. I'm Payton, and this is my twin—"

"Emma."

We both said it at the same time.

"I thought *I* was supposed to say Emma," Emma said.

"You did say that," Lakiya from tech crew nodded.

"Ack, I'm so nervous, I keep screwing up!" I said. "Why am I so nervous?"

"You're nervous because you care," Nick said. "This is not only your first VOGS cast as a traveling correspondent, but the first on-site VOGS cast ever."

"And I want to be great!" I said. "I want this to be the best, most fun, greatest segment on VOGS ever!"

"Besides our big fight," Emma added. "Broadcast live in front of the whole school."

"That *is* a classic," Lakiya said nodding.

"See, I'm willing to humiliate myself again for the cause of a good VOGS cast!" I wailed.

I was startled by somebody clapping behind me.

"Brava! *Bravissimo!*" It was Mrs. Burkle. I didn't know she was there. "I love the commitment, the intensity of emotion, the willingness to put yourself out there for the sake of our viewers on VOGS. Nice start, Payton."

"Oh," I said. "Um, thanks."

"Now, I don't want you to go too far," Mrs. Burkle said. "This isn't a reality show for television invested in embarrassing people for the sake of ratings. However, a dramatic VOGS cast is welcome."

"We're planning a competition," Emma told Mrs. Burkle. "The triplets are out scouting locations right now. That should bring some drama."

"Carry on!" Mrs. Burkle said happily.

"That should make you feel good," Nick said, smiling at me. "Plus, remember, we'll edit later. Okay, you're on in five . . . four . . . three . . . two . . ."

"We're live from Multipalooza! A festival for twins, triplets, and multiple identicals! I'm Payton, and this is *my* identical twin . . ."

"Emma!" Emma said. "Have you ever wondered what's it like to have an identical twin or triplet? We'll be asking some of these thousands of people here."

Nick swung the camera out toward the crowd, then back toward us.

"And if you *haven't* wondered that," I said, "perhaps you'll enjoy watching your fellow students humiliate themselves! Because I think that's going to happen today! Emma and I are challenging three of our newest Gecko classmates to an identicals competition."

The triplets sauntered over to us and waved, saluted, and grinned at the camera.

"We're the SUPERTWINS!" they said.

"SuperTwins are like twins, but better because . . ."

". . . there's three of us."

"Later, we'll be performing onstage here at Multi-palooza, but first we need to take down the twins who AREN'T super."

The camera panned to Emma and me.

"You can't talk to Emma and Payton like that!" an unexpected voice shouted out. Mason and Jason ran in front of us and got in the triplets' faces. "TWINS RULE!"

"Guys," Emma whispered. "It's okay. It's just for fun."

"GO, SUPERTWINS!" Sydney and Cashmere waved their signs around. "TRIPLETS RULE!"

"Multipalooza Twins Versus Triplets," I said loudly, "begins now."

"And . . . cut!" Nick said. "That was great!"

"Very dramatic!" Mrs. Burkle said.

"Great. Moving forward, we have fifteen minutes before our first competitive event," Emma said.

Emma had agreed to be in charge of our schedule, for obvious reasons. We'd had a quick discussion with the triplets about which events we would compete against each other in. (We each had veto power over one event. We'd used ours to rule out Multipaloo-Karaoke; they'd used theirs to rule out Multipaloo Spelling Bee. Thankfully. Obviously that was Emma's suggestion.)

"Let's interview some multiples, then," I decided. We walked into the main area, and there were hundreds! Thousands! Jillions! Of us. Where would I even start? It was overwhelming.

"I guess just ask someone if you can interview them, and I'll be ready with the camera," Nick said. "I'll stick close to you."

Hee hee hee. The thought of Nick sticking close to me was also a little overwhelming. He was so cute and— focus, Payton! Okay.

I went up to twin girls who looked about my age. They had black curly hair and were wearing matching outfits—but in different colors!

"Hi," I said. "May we interview you for a school video?"

"Okay," the girls said.

"Can you introduce yourselves and tell me why you came to Multipalooza?"

"I'm Gia," one said.

"I'm Ria," the other said. "We're here because it's amazing to see all of these people who look alike, like us."

"Sometimes we feel like freaks, but not here!" Gia laughed. "That moment when people see two of you and their eyes get wide and you know they're thinking, THREE of those crazy girls?"

Wait. Three? Sure enough, a third identical came over to them.

"Oh!" I laughed. "Surprise triplets."

"Who's she?" The third eyed me up and down. "Is this for TV?"

"Um, no, for our school video," I told her.

"Waste of time," the third one scoffed. "Let's go."

Gia and Ria both mouthed "Sorry!" and followed her away.

"Gee, can you tell who's the Dominant Twin there?" Emma said. "Yowch!"

The next twins, boys who were there all the way from Texas, were way nicer.

Then I interviewed other twins, triplets, and even quadruplets!

"We have time for one more interview before we head to our event," Emma said.

I looked around for unique people and—

"Over there." I found some I definitely wanted to interview. They were two girls and a boy around Mason and Jason's age. They stood out not only because of their bright red hair but because they were dressed up in costumes. Not identically, but definitely a theme: zombies. They agreed to be interviewed.

"You guys stand out in the crowd," Emma said on camera. "Tell us about yourselves."

"We're triplets. I'm Tate," one of the girls said. She had long, wavy red hair, white face makeup, and fake blood the same shade of red dripping down her face. "I'm a zombie. I want your *braaaiiinnns*."

"I'm Hadley," the other girl said. Her curly red hair was under a sparkling crown. Fake blood dripped down her face and pink princess dress. "I'm a zombie princess. I also want your *braaaiiinnns*."

"I'm Jasper," said the boy with short red hair and extra fake gore to go with his fake blood on his face and arms. "I'm a zombie, too. *Braaaiiinnns*."

"May I ask why you dressed up today?" I tried not to laugh.

"Dressed up?" Tate asked. "I don't know what you mean. We're zombies who specialize in eating twins, and triplets' brains. Can we have yours?"

"Um, no," Now I did laugh. I thanked them.

"Mason and Jason would love those kids," Emma said. "Okay, I think we definitely got enough unique interviews for now. It's time for our first Twins Versus Triplets Challenge!"

Twenty

COMPETITION TIME

"GO, Twins!"

"GO, SuperTwins!"

I could hear our fans and our nemeses chanting as Payton and I were in the girls' bathroom. We were getting ready to compete in our first Multipalooza event. Since we'd been wearing our VOGS blazerly attire, we needed to change. Fortunately, we'd brought track pants so we'd be comfy for the ride home.

"Here you go, girls!" Mrs. Burkle's voice echoed in the ladies' room. "Courtesy of Multipalooza and the triplets' aunt, who was working at the T-shirt booth! Catch!"

A red T-shirt flew over the top of the stall. I unrolled it and pulled it on over my tank top. I looked down and read the white letters:

MULTIPALOOZA!

It was time for a competition! I needed a competition. It had been too long since I felt that feeling in my veins, in my brains. It was time to challenge myself and win, win, win!

As I gave myself my pep talk, I did my deep-breathing exercises. I did my yoga focus pose. I stretched.

"Emma, are you ready?" Payton called out, still in the stall.

"I've given myself a pep talk, I did my deep-breathing exercises, I did my focus yoga pose, and I stretched," I answered. "Yes, Payton. YES! I AM READY! Woot! Let's do it!"

I gave a little fist pump in the air.

"Um, I just meant are you ready, as in are you dressed?" Payton asked.

"Oh," I said. "Yes. Yes, I am."

"Then can you help me?" she said. "My earring is caught in my tank top."

I pushed the stall door open and—

"Ack!" Payton said, her head sideways. She jerked her head up and rrriiip! I watched as the earring ripped the strap of her tank top.

"I didn't know you were just going to bust in here!" she said.

"Well, you asked for help," I said indignantly. "I thought that meant help me by entering, not by mental telepathy outside the stall. Okay, hang on."

"I *am* hanging on," Payton said, pointing to her hand holding her tank strap.

I could take care of that. I reached into my tote bag and into the zipped-up case of supplies. There it was! Duct tape! And safety scissors.

"Did you know that duct tape was first invented in World War Two to help the American military?" I asked Payton as she wrapped her strap.

"Yes," Payton said. "Because you told me that. And do you know *when* you told me that?"

I suddenly remembered.

"The Janitor's Closet!" we both said at the same time.

"The start of my middle school career." Payton sighed. "Fortunately, it got better. And fortunately, my tank top is better too! Yeah!"

❀ 164 ❀

She pulled on her red T-shirt. She went over to the mirror and pulled her hair up in a high ponytail just like mine. I stood next to her. We stood side by side, dressed exactly the same.

"If I shrunk down to be one inch shorter," Payton said, slouching down, "we'd be pretty much exactly the same."

"And if your hair were less shiny," I responded.

"Hey!" Payton swatted me.

"Shiny, shiny—" I started.

"—double the shiny," she finished. "Hmmm, is that our rallying cry?"

"No," I said. "It's . . . go, GECKOS! *Twin!*" I punched the air. And added a little jump.

Time to go show those triplets what the Mills Twins can do!

"Emma," Payton said. "We will soon be on film. Please don't do that again. It's embarrassing to both of us."

"Okay." I shrugged. "If you think my team spirit is embarrassing, perhaps you might want to know you have yellow duct tape sticking out of your T-shirt."

"Eep!" Payton shoved it back in the neck of her shirt.

"I have an idea. Let's *both* try not to embarrass ourselves or each other," I said, checking the schedule. "Although now that I see our first challenge, that could prove difficult. It's called Dizzy Ploozy."

"What the heck is Dizzy Ploozy?" Payton asked.

Challenge #1: Dizzy Ploozy

It turned out that Dizzy Ploozy involved putting our foreheads down on a Wiffle ball bat and walking in a circle around and around the bat fifteen times. Then running across the field to the finish line blindfolded.

"O-kay," I said, then geared myself up for the competition.

"Be careful of your vibulator issues," Payton said with a smile.

"That's vestibular," I told her. "And now I can prove to everyone that I don't have any."

A girl with a Multipalooza staff T-shirt brought us each Wiffle ball bats and blindfolds. Other staffers handed out supplies to all the multiples who were competing.

There were a lot of them.

"We're in it to win it," I reminded my twin. "Or at least to beat those triplets."

"Ready." Payton looked determined. We pulled the blindfolds over our eyes.

A man announced the rules over a microphone. The winning team would be the first team to have two of its members cross the finish line.

"On your marks . . . get set . . . ," the announcer said. "Go!"

I rested my forehead on the bat and started circling.

"One! Two!" the crowd started counting. The loud crowd. A lot of people were watching us.

I used my calm, centered, focused attention and breathed steadily in and out as I went around and around.

"Fourteen! Fifteen!"

And I was off! Off balance, that is. I hesitantly took a step. And another. Whoa. I was in a world of darkness that rotated rapidly.

I soldiered forth. Another step. And then I heard people yelling.

"Payton! Wrong way! Payton! Turn around!"

I didn't recognize those voices. Boy, people were really rooting for us.

"Payton!" I said. "Turn around!"

"I haven't gone anywhere yet!" Payton shrieked. "I'm too dizzy!"

That made no sense. But whatever.

"Just breathe and walk!" I yelled.

Suddenly I heard shouts.

"Emma! Turn around! Wrong way!"

Oops. I must have gotten mixed up while talking. I turned 180 degrees and step-by-step, I was walking! And then I was practically jogging! I could do this!

"Emma! Watch out to your left!" someone yelled. I heard other people being told, "Left! Right! Get back up!" But I just focused on my name and veered to the right.

"No, Emma! Go left!"

"Payton! Go right!"

What? I was getting mixed messages. I stumbled left, then I confidently went forward.

"Payton, right! Right, Payton!"

Were they telling my twin to go right or was she *doing* it right? I hoped it was the latter, because I HAD to be near the finish line—

Wham!

I collided with something and fell backward on my rear end.

"And the winning team is . . . ," the announcer was saying. "And second place is about to cross the line . . ."

Ergh. We'd lost. I pulled up my blindfold and saw—
Payton. She was sitting on the ground next to me, with
her blindfold off.

"We crashed," she said. "Into each other."

"I don't get it," I complained. "I was following the
crowd's directions!"

"So was I," said Payton. We helped each other up
and wobble-walked toward our friends on the sidelines.

"I guess the triplets won this one," Payton said.

"Or not," I said, starting to smile. All three boys were
lying on the field. I stepped over one of them.

"What happened?" I looked down innocently.

"I couldn't make it past twelve," one triplet admitted. "And my brothers were too dizzy and gave up."

Gave up?

"So nobody wins!" I exclaimed. "Team Mills and
Team SuperTwins are tied zero-zero!"

"Ha!" I said to Payton as we continued on. "They
must have looked so embarrassing. At least we got somewhere!"

"Yeah," Payton said. "And Nick was filming, so they
got that all on tape!"

We reached our friends.

Who were, for some reason, looking at us and laughing hysterically.

"What's so funny?" I asked.

"You two are . . ." Cashmere tried to talk. "You both are . . ." She couldn't finish, she was giggling so much.

"We're what?" Payton and I said at the same time.

"You're wearing the wrong T-shirt!" Sydney was doubled over laughing.

Huh?

"We're wearing matching Multipalooza shirts," I said, confused.

"Turn around," Ox said, grinning.

Payton turned around, and that's when I saw it. On her back, in black letters, it read:

EMMA

"Oh no," I groaned. "Mine says PAYTON, doesn't it?" I craned my neck and looked. Yes. Yes, it did.

"We didn't see that there was anything on the back of the shirts!" Payton wailed.

"You two mixed *yourselves* up. You didn't even know which one of you was which!" Ox said, trying not to crack up. And failing.

"I could barely keep the camera from shaking, I was laughing so hard," Nick said, gasping for breath.

Mason and Jason simply rolled around on the ground, laughing.

Okay, fine. Let's move forward, shall we?

Challenge #2: Multipaloo-Trivia

This next one, we've got locked up.

I'd been on a game show recently—in Hollywood! I'd done quite well. Sure, I'd been covered with green ooze at the end, but still! This time, I planned to do even better. Payton and I *had* to win this one.

"Welcome to *Multipaloo-Trivia*!" the announcer said into a microphone. "We have our panel of contestants lined up."

Now *this* felt like a real competition. We were onstage, in seats facing the audience, like at a spelling bee or a Mathletes competition. It felt like home to me.

"Emma," Payton whispered. "This feels really weird being up here, with all these people staring at us."

Apparently, it didn't feel like home to Payton.

"Payton," I whispered. "You've been onstage for plays and even off-Broadway. You'll be just fine."

"But they couldn't see us so close up. Don't sneeze

or sweat." Payton tilted her head. What was she talking about? I turned around and—

Yikes! An enormous movie-theater-style screen had come down behind us, and yes, there we were. Live and in color. Perhaps HD. As the camera panned across the panel, I could see two of the triplets' smug grins, large and supersized. I planned to wipe those smiles right off their faces. Oh, and then I saw Payton's giant face and then the side of my head, looking at the screen behind me.

Oops. Live camera. I spun around and smiled at the audience. A nice, confident, winning smile.

The announcer announced, "Let's give a cheer for Team Number One: Dexter and Oliver—the Super-Twins!"

Dexter and Oliver stood up and waved.

From the audience, Sydney and Cashmere (and okay, maybe one or more other naive girls) squealed at them. Asher was standing next to Cashmere, and he gave her a high five.

Then the announcer continued.

Team #2: Random Twins!

Team #3: The Mills Twins!

Team #4: Oh boy. It was two of the black-curly-haired triplets Payton had interviewed. Gia, Ria, and

Mean Girl. Mean Girl gave me a squinty look. I gave her my competition stare. Oh, it's on, Mean Triplet. It's on!

Payton and I waved at the audience. I could see Ox give me a thumbs-up and Nick with his camera on. Mason and Jason were jumping up and down.

"We'll ask you questions, and whoever hits the buzzer first gets a point!"

I took a deep breath. I focused. I went into competition mode.

Question #1: How many twins live in the United States today?

I hit the button.

"Four and a half million!" I answered.

"And that is correct!" the announcer said. "One point for the Mills Twins! Next question: What is the scientific study of multiple births called?"

BAM!

"Gemellology," I said. "From the Latin *gemellus* for 'twin' and the Greek *logos* for 'science.'"

Correct!

"What is the name of the classic movie twins who—"
Uh-oh.

Slam! Mean Triplet beat me. "Parent Trap!"

"Yay, Lia!" Gia or Ria cheered her on.

Team #4 was obviously my competition. I was ready for the next question.

Bam! Mine. *Slam!* Mean Triplets.

The rest of the game was a blur. Questions were fast and furious.

"And the final tally is: Team Number One has five points," the announcer said. "Team Number Two has ten, Team Number Four has sixty, and the winners are : . .

"With eighty-five points . . . Team Number Three! The Mills Twins!"

Oh. Yeah. I could conquer two sets of triplets today. If you were gonna mess with the Mills twins, you were going down.

"Um, Emma?" Payton piped up. "Can you stop with the victory awkward-dance? We're about to be on film."

The VOGS crew ran over and started filming us. I smiled my best competition smile at the VOGS camera.

"Twins, one; boy-band-wanna-be triplets, zero," I said. Payton and I did our twin hand-clap-slap.

Heh heh heh.

Okay. No time to rest on our laurels.

"The momentum is in our favor," I said to Payton. "The next competition is *OURS*! Woo-hoo! Woo—"

"The next competition is the Three-Legged Race," Payton interrupted me.

Woo . . . uh-oh.

Twenty-one

IN COMPETITION

"Let's see if you twins can even walk without falling over!" The triplets were shouting smack at us at the starting line of the Three-Legged Race. I was leaning over, wrapping a rope around one of my legs and one of Emma's.

"Who told the triplets we were totally uncoordinated?" Emma grumbled. "I bet it was Sydney. Maybe Jazmine James filled them in about my vestibular disorder."

"Or maybe it was that the triplets first saw you walk into a door, then fall, and smack your head against the ground?" I reminded her.

"Okay, the rope is tied," I said, pulling it tightly. "Let's practice. We have to wrap our arms around each other and coordinate."

We both stood up. I was facing one way, Emma was facing the other. We waddled around . . . in a circle. Wait a minute.

"Aren't we supposed to be facing the same way?" I asked. Before Emma could answer, we toppled over onto the grass. I looked up to see the tech girl filming us, and Nick laughing behind her.

"Cut!" Nick said. "Um, you tied both of your left legs together."

"You're supposed to tie my left leg and your *right* leg," Emma said.

Oops.

"We're doomed," I told Emma.

"Don't give up," Emma said. "Don't ever give up. But first, get up."

Two of the triplets, along with about a hundred other people, were already tied together, practicing walking in unison. We struggled to untie ourselves, then retied us together the correct way. When I stood up, Emma put her arm around me, and we got ourselves balanced.

"Participants, line up!" a referee yelled out.

Emma and I stumbled to the starting line.

"Start with your left, then pace yourself to a rhythm," Emma said. "Like, twinkle, twinkle, little star; left, right, left, right . . ."

"Twin-kle, Twin-kle!" I brightened up. "Our twin song. We're going to twin-kle like stars!"

The triplets team walk-hopped up and stood next to us in line.

"Did you tie the correct legs together this time?" one of the triplets asked us.

Rats, they saw that.

"Ignore them," Emma whispered. "They're just trying to throw us off. Stay cool under the pressure."

"On your marks," the announcer called out. "Get set . . ."

"We go left first, right?" I asked Emma.

"Right," Emma said.

Right? Right leg first or right that I was correct? I opened my mouth to ask Emma, but before I had a chance—

"Go!"

I jumped forward on my right foot. The rope pulled tightly, and Emma gave a little yelp as we lurched sideways and oof! I fell right on top of Emma. I looked up to see the triplets smoothly blowing right past us, with the rest of the hundreds of people.

Triplets:1, Twins:1

We were all tied up.

It all would come down to the Tug-of-War.

Challenge #3: Tug-of-War

The tiebreaker.

The Multipalooza Twins Versus Triplets Challenge would come down to a tug-of-war. We all walked toward the field where our Tug-of-War was scheduled to take place.

Nick was already there setting up his video camera. Ox, Sydney, and Cashmere were standing near him.

"Emma! Payton! Emma! Payton!"

I turned around to see Mason and Jason bouncing up to us. They were both face-painted to look like lizards. They were also holding balloon sculpture swords.

"Looks like you guys are having a good time," I said to them.

"Guess what? Guess what?" Mason said, jumping all over in excitement. "I won a cake in the Cake Walk!

And a goldfish in the Ping-Pong Ball Throw! I named him Mrs. Slurples!"

"I didn't win anything," Jason said, frowning. "He's winning everything."

"I've been there," I said to Jason empathetically. "Emma is always winning things and not so much me."

"Well, Payton and I are both going to win in a few minutes—together," Emma said emphatically. "Mason and Jason, your dad is waving you over."

"We'll be cheering you on!" Mason said. "Be a winner—like me! Not Jason!"

Jason trudged off the field.

"Emma," I said. "I'm not entirely clear on how this is going to work. Even if it's only two triplets against us, there's no way we can win."

"When I feel like all hope is lost in a competition, I think of ways to psych out the other competitors," Emma said. "Like when Jazmine James answered 'parabola' in Mathletes, and I said, 'Sorry, but it's inverse parabola.'"

Well. Emma certainly had more practice in competitions than I did. I'd have to trust she knew what she was doing.

"Oh, look!" Emma said. "Ready to be humiliated?"

The triplets walked up to us, grinning.

"We're going to pull you into Loserville!" a triplet replied. "Multipla-losers!"

"You don't stand a chance, Twin-kies," another said. "Get it, TWIN-kies?"

"We have a few tricks up our sleeve. We use our brains, Subtriplicates!" Emma said. "Get it, SubTRIPLicates?"

I wasn't the only one who looked confused. The triplets did as well.

"What's a subtriplicate?" I whispered to Emma. "Is it really bad?"

"It's when a ratio is expressed by its cube root," Emma whispered back. "I'm trying to psych them out with our brainpower."

"Yeah!" I yelled. "You guys are subtriplicates!"

"What are you talking about?" a triplet asked us.

"You're not intelligent enough to understand, you Triploblasty," Emma shot back. She turned to me and whispered. "That means having three germ layers: ectoderm, mesoderm, and endoderm. Ha! Germs as an insult! I'm good."

Well, she was definitely good at pumping herself up. And confusing the rest of us.

"Attention, participants!" an announcer announced.

"All Tug-of-War teams please report to the sign-in table!"

We followed the Triplets up to the table. And that's where things got really confused. "Team member names?" a woman behind the table asked.

"Dexter and Asher," one of the triplets said.

"And . . . ?" the woman asked.

"And . . . versus Emma and Payton?" Emma leaned forward to tell her.

"Your team is Dexter, Asher, Emma, Payton, and . . . ," the woman said.

"No, no!" We practically all yelled.

"We're competing *against* them," a triplet said.

"You need six people on each team," the woman said.

We do?

"And quickly, because you only have three minutes for sign-ups," the woman said.

"Quick, we need more people," the triplets said.

"Ox!" I said to Emma. "We need Ox! He'll win this for us!"

"He does have strong muscles," Emma said dreamily. Then she snapped back.

"Well, that's not really fair competition because then it's not Twins Versus Triplets," a triplet complained.

"You're right," Emma suddenly said. "Okay, we'll go round up official multiples. Meet us back here in two minutes."

The triplets looked at one another and took off. Emma and I ran too.

"Um, Emma," I said, jogging beside her. "Where are we going?"

Emma stopped. "I have no idea. I just couldn't give up and give the triplets the satisfaction. But we don't really know anybody else here, do we?"

Emma and I looked at each other. We looked around. Nope.

"Well," Emma said. "I guess that's that."

"Payton! Emma! We're going to cheer for you in the Tug-of-War!" Mason and Jason ran up to us.

"Sorry, boys," I said. "Looks like we won't be competing."

"Unless we just ask random people in the crowd," Emma suggested.

"We'll be on the team!" Mason said. "We're tough and strong!"

"Not saying you're not," Emma said carefully. "But we'd be competing against the triplets and whoever else they find. Thanks anyway."

"You think we can't handle it?" Jason puffed up his chest.

"Um . . ." I thought fast. "We still need two more people on the team in about thirty seconds, so I don't think it will work out."

Mason and Jason looked at each other and walked away.

"I feel bad," I said. "It was nice of them to offer. Do you think their feelings are hurt? Are they off crying somewhere?"

"No," said Emma slowly. "No, they're definitely not crying."

I turned around to see Mason and Jason half-dragging two people toward us, followed by another one.

"We have our team!" Mason said. "Two more people! They said yes!"

Um. The two more people were two of the triplets we'd interviewed before. The ones who were about Mason and Jason's age. The ones in zombie costumes. Still in zombie costumes.

"What do we do?" I said under my breath to Emma. "We're going to be laughed off the stage. That is, after we get pulled into Loserville."

"We're so excited!" the zombie girl said. "I can't

believe that *we* can help *you* guys out! The 'Shiny, Shiny Double the Shiny' TV stars!"

"Tate recognized you from the shampoo commercial after we talked to you," the zombie boy said. "Can we have your autographs after we do the Tug-of-War?"

"I can't wait to tell everyone in school we were on a team with television stars!" Tate said.

Emma and I looked at each other.

"We better hurry," Emma sighed. "So we don't miss the sign-ups."

"You have got to be kidding," a triplet said when we'd regrouped at the sign-in table.

"We're gonna pull you guys across the line so fast, you won't know what hit you!" Mason said to them.

"Yeah!" said Tate, the zombie-costumed girl. "In your face!"

"Wait a minute," one of the triplets suddenly said. "Nobody told me we have to compete against zombies. What if you try to eat my brains?"

He recoiled in mock horror.

"That's Asher," Emma whispered to me. "He's actually pretty nice."

I guess that was one good thing about our team of

nine-year-olds. The triplets couldn't really trash-talk us too hard.

"Well, who's on your team?" Jason challenged them.

All three triplets lined up. Then a set of large twin guys in matching T-shirts with rock bands on them.

"Wait, you need six people," Jason pointed out.

Then another large guy with a rock band T-shirt joined them.

We were doomed.

"I'm here! I'm here!" Cashmere pushed through the crowd.

Cashmere?

"You can't do Tug-of-War," I said.

Cashmere pulled a little spray bottle out of her hoodie pocket and started spritzing the triplets' team.

"Hey!" they all yelped. "What are you doing?"

"Sydney didn't want you guys to be too stinky for the dance, so she told me to spray you with this scented body spray." Cashmere skipped away.

"Are we glittering?" a triplet looked at his arm. "Was that body glitter?"

"Yep," a big rock band guy said. "We're glittering. Smell pretty sweet too."

"All Tug-of-War teams, please report to your assigned station!"

"Good luck, Glittering Triplets," Emma said, smiling at them.

We all headed over to where the teams were and split up at the ends of the rope. Nick and the tech crew came over to film us.

"Go, SuperTwins!" Sydney held up her sign.

"Go, Geckos!" Mrs. Burkle called out.

"There are Geckos on both sides," I called to Mrs. Burkle.

"Then I'm rooting for both of you!" she said. "And for good television!"

"Go, Zombies!" The zombie princess had brought her parents.

Our team lined up at one end of the rope.

"The strongest of us should be the anchor," Jason said. We all looked at one another. We were Emma, me, and four nine-year-olds.

"I guess that's me!" Jason said, flexing. He grabbed the back of the rope as we all sighed.

"Shoulda been me," Mason grumbled. "I'll be up front and intimidate them with my scary face."

"We have scary faces too!" the zombie kids growled

and roared. Oh yes, our team was going to be . . .
intimidating.

We faced off:

**TRIPLET—ROCK GUY—ROCK GUY—
TRIPLET—ROCK GUY—TRIPLET**
VERSUS
**MASON—ME—ZOMBIE PRINCESS—
ZOMBIE BOY—EMMA—JASON**

"All teams," the announcer yelled. "On your
marks . . ."

I held on to the rope tight.

"Get set . . . GO!"

"PUUUuuuullll!" Jason yelled. And we pulled! I
pulled as hard as I could. And for one split second, I
thought we were holding our ground.

Then the other team pulled.

Uh-oh.

My feet tried to dig into the grass, but I felt myself
slipping forward. We were losing ground fast.

"We're losing! I'm almost over the line already!"
Mason sounded panicky. In front of me, I could see him
pulling so hard that his cap was falling off.

And underneath his cap? It was something . . . moving! And then I saw it.

"Mason," I said, through clenched teeth. "Did you bring Mascot?" The gecko? He brought his pet gecko?

Before he had a chance to answer, Mascot saw something glint in the sunlight. It was the arms of the triplet in the front! Covered in sparkly body glitter. The gecko leaped toward the sparkly glittered arm . . .

"Mascot!" Mason yelped. "Get back in my hat!"

"He had Mascot in his *hat*?" I heard Emma say. We were still holding on!

"In a special climate-controlled small cage that I invented that fits in his hat," Jason answered. Still. Holding. The rope.

"Impressive," Emma said. "PULL!"

Meanwhile—

"AGH! WHAT IS ON ME?" the triplet in the front was shrieking. "GET THAT OFF ME!"

The triplet dropped the rope and started trying to shoo Mascot off of him. Mascot jumped to his head. The triplet started screaming and running in circles. Mason chased after him.

This is where I hoped that the other team would be

distracted, allowing us to pull them toward us, and we would WIN in a stunning underdog upset.

That did not happen. Even without a triplet, we were YANKED forward over the finish line.

We all tumbled forward on top of one another: me, Emma, Jason, and two zombie children. Sigh.

"We win!" the other team was hooting and yelling. "We win!"

"Good job, dudes." The triplets high-fived the random rocker dudes, who grinned and left, victorious. Dexter, Asher, and Oliver ran up to us.

"We win! We win the Multipalooza Twins Versus Triplets Challenge!"

Emma

Twenty-two

AFTER COMPETITION

"You win." I sighed, holding out my hand to shake. Ergh, I hated saying those words. But you win some and you lose some. A hard lesson I'd had to learn these past few months. But now I knew—it's not all about winning; it's also how you play the game.

Two triplets still danced around hooting. One triplet shook my hand.

"Good effort," Asher said. "Well, interesting effort anyway."

"I've got Mascot back," Mason said, and patted his hat. "He's okay, but he's bummed that we lost."

"I'm hungry," one of the zombies said. "Let's go eat."

"Brains?" Jason asked her.

"Nah, funnel cakes. Want to get some too?" the zombie asked the boys.

"Yeah!" Mason's face brightened.

"Let's go ask Mom and Dad!" Jason said, and they ran off.

"Mason and Jason and zombies," I said. "A perfect combination."

Meanwhile, the triplets were still celebrating. "You have to wear the T-shirts we pick!" they said, laughing. "And say 'Triplets are better' on the school video show!"

"SuperTwins rule!" Sydney cheered.

"Brava! Brava!" Mrs. Burkle came up to us. "This is going to be *fantastic* television. The underdogs in their eye-catching fashions! The moment that the lizard jumps onto the other team, and that team member shrieks like a small child."

One of the two triplets stopped dancing.

"I didn't *shriek like a small child*," he said.

"So dramatic! Such excitement! Great job, Payton," Mrs. Burkle said. "This could possibly be our best VOGS cast yet."

"Thanks!" Payton squeaked. "Everyone did a great

job. Emma, Lakiya, tech, even the triplets . . ."

"Payton," I said, and hugged her, "remember how much you wanted to have a great VOGS cast? You came up with this idea, and you did it!"

Payton was beaming.

"Excuse me." A man in a Multipalooza Staff T-shirt came up to us. "Please go back to your tug-of-war rope for the next round."

"We just went," Emma told him.

"Which team won?" the man asked. "The winning team gets to continue against a new team."

"We're the winning team!" the triplets all said. "But we don't have half of our team! Those guys are gone!"

"Well, you'll have to be disqualified then," the staff guy said.

"Yeah, well, the SuperTwins have to perform soon anyway," one of the triplets said. "Let's head over to the main stage, bros."

"Uh-oh. I think I'm going to puke," a different triplet said. He was turning green. Must be Asher.

"What's wrong?" Payton asked.

"It's just . . . just . . . I have stage fright," he blurted out. "Okay? I'm nervous. There. I said it."

His brothers looked at him.

"Wimp! Wuss!" one of them jeered. "Get over it, Oliver!"

Wait a minute. Oliver?

"Oliver, you're nervous too?" the triplet I realized was Asher asked. "*I'm* nervous as all heck."

"Oh, don't be nervous, Asher." Cashmere put her hand on his arm. "You're going to be wonderful!"

"Really?" Asher turned to her and blushed.

"Hey, I'm the one who's nervous," Oliver protested. "I'm the one who thinks we're going to look like idiots and stink up the stage."

"Toughen up, bros," Dexter said.

"Yeah, toughen up," Sydney said scornfully. "And don't think you can use puking as an excuse to get out of the dance tonight either."

Now Dexter looked a little ill too.

"Guys!" Nick jogged over with Ox behind him. "I just saw Mason and Jason. They've entered a contest, and the VOGS crew is setting up to film it."

Final Multipalooza Competition (but one that doesn't involve us): Multipaloo-Limbo

"Get ready to limbo!" the announcer announced. "How low can you go?!"

"Do you see them?" Payton asked. We were standing with Ox, Nick, and Lakiya on the sidelines. I looked for Mason and Jason in the long line of younger kids.

"There they are," Nick said, turning his video camera toward the end of the line. "I can see them with my zoom lens. They're right behind two of the zombies."

That narrowed it down. I spotted them too. They were both hopping up and down from excitement.

"Mason! Jason!" I yelled. They turned and waved when they spotted us.

"Multipaloo-Limbo is TWIN-bo," the announcer said. "You have to hold hands with your twin partner the whole time. If either of you touches the rope or the ground, you are eliminated."

"Mason and Jason working together?" I said. "This is going to be interesting."

The music started, and the line started moving. At first, the rope was so high, most of the kids practically could walk under it. Mason and Jason held hands and went under easily.

"Go, Mason and Jason!" we all yelled.

Then the rope lowered, and some kids were disqualified.

"Mason and Jason are still in it," Ox said. "So are the

zombies, although I'm thinking the long princess dress is going to be a stumbling block."

Ox was right. The princess zombie went down in the next round. We all cheered for them as they left the field.

"They're getting to the head of the line," Nick said.

"Go, Mason! Go, Jason!" we shouted. I was watching so intently, I didn't notice some people come up next to me at first.

It was the triplets, Sydney, and Cashmere.

"How are Mason and Jason doing?" Cashmere asked.

"They're still in." I pointed. "You can see Mason's red hat. They're almost up."

We all waited until the boys got almost to the rope, then we exploded.

"Go, Mason! Go, Jason!"

"GO, LITTLE DUDES!" one of the triplets yelled.

"Go, Geckos!" Sydney called out. She did some complicated kick-jump cheer move, probably to show off for the triplets. But they were busy watching the limbo game.

And we were all watching as Mason and Jason made it under the rope!

"Yes!" we were all screaming. I held up my hand, and Ox high-fived it.

We watched as the line got smaller and smaller each round. Kids were dropping like flies. But not Mason and Jason! They held hands and bent backward, under the rope again.

Now we were all jumping up and down.

"Little dudes are ROCKING this," a triplet said.

I looked over at them.

"It's nice of you to cheer them on," I said.

"They're cool little dudes," Oliver (Dexter?) said.

"We're all Geckos," Sydney said. "We're all on the same team. GO, GECKOS!"

It was now down to about five teams. And Mason and Jason were still in it! Then the line was moving, but Mason and Jason suddenly stopped.

"It looks like there's a problem," Ox said, squinting.

"Mason is rubbing his hat," Nick said. "I can see with my zoom lens. Maybe he's afraid his hat is giving him extra height?"

"Why can't he just take off his hat?" a triplet asked.

Oh. OH!!! I knew why!

"I'll be right back!" I said. I raced across the limbo field. I ran up to one of the people with "Multipalooza Staff" on her shirt and explained the situation. She let me run out to the boys.

"Mason!" I said. "I'll take it! I'll take the hat!"

"Emma," he said. "You know what's in it, right?"

"Yes," I said. "I'll take good care of Mascot. We're cheering you on!"

I carried the hat carefully across the field. I peeked inside to make sure Mascot was okay. Yep, the lizard was safe and sound in the hat cage that Jason had made for him.

"Well, Mascot," I said. "Go, Geckos, right?"

Mascot winked an eye and stuck out his tongue at me. I shuddered.

"Emma!" Payton was calling out to me. "Look!"

I walked faster and rejoined my sister and our friends. Other teams were falling or touching the rope.

"Mason was worried about Mascot in his hat," I said, holding the hat carefully.

"The gecko?" one of the triplets said. "That thing is cool."

"Want to hold him?" I offered. Excellent. He took the hat out of my hands.

"Hey, little gecko dude," he said gently into the hat. "I'm Oliver. Aren't you a good boy."

Well. That was helpful.

I turned around to see that Mason and Jason were reaching the front of the line, and there was only one team ahead of them. Only one other team. Oh wow! It was down to just them and Mason and Jason!

We all watched as the other team bent over backward and limbo'd toward the rope and then—*splat!* They fell!

"Oh my gosh, oh my gosh," Sydney said. "If Mason and Jason make it, they'll win! I'm so nervous!"

She reached out and grabbed my hand. Wow. Sydney held on to my hand for support and camaraderie. We really all were a team. Then she looked over.

"Ick," she said. "I thought I was standing next to a triplet."

"Oh, let's cheer together, Sydney," I said. "We're all on the same team. GO, GECKOS!"

"Go, Geckos!" Sydney yelled. Then she did some elaborate cheer jump that practically knocked me over. We might be on the same team, but she was still Sydney.

"Okay," Nick said. "They're up."

"Eeee!" Payton squealed, her hands covering her eyes. "I can't look! Tell me what happens!"

"GO, MASON AND JASON!" I yelled. I looked at the triplets and grinned. "Go, little dudes!"

"GO, LITTLE DUDES!" we all yelled together.

"They're bending backward," Nick reported for Payton. "Farther, farther, and . . ."

THEY DID IT! Mason and Jason limbo'd under the rope!!! They won! They won!

WOO!! We were all cheering and jumping up and down! Everyone was high-fiving one another! Even the triplets! I jumped up, and Ox caught me in a hug!

Woo-hoo!

Mason and Jason accepted a trophy from the announcer. They turned to us and started waving. I could read Mason's lips: "Emma! I WON SOMETHING!"

Go, little dudes.

Payton

Twenty-three

IN OUR BEDROOM, FOUR HOURS LATER

I looked at myself in the mirror. My hair was piled on my head in a soft updo. Little curls fell along my face. I loved my hair! I also loved my dress. The jewel-toned sapphire blue looked nice against the slight tan I'd gotten today at Multipalooza. My tights also covered up the bruises I'd gotten from the last round of Tug-of-War.

Which, by the way, we had lost. We'd competed with the triplets and one of the Rock Guys but . . . the other team consisted of five massive teenage boys and their equally massive younger sister.

I smiled at myself in the mirror. What was important

was that we'd had fun. And also, according to Mrs. Burkle, I'd done an incredible VOGS cast. Squee!

Suddenly, I was seeing double! No, not really. Emma was standing behind me in the mirror. She had also put her hair in an updo. She looked amazing in her silvery dress. Her tights covered up the scrape she'd gotten when I'd landed on her in the Three-Legged Race.

"Emma," I breathed. "We're going to our very first dance."

Squee!

Double squee!

Emma

Twenty-four

AT THE AUTUMN DANCE!

Wow.

Our school gym had been turned into an autumn wonderland. Hundreds of leaves—red, orange, yellow, and green—decorated the walls. Red and gold streamers crisscrossed the ceiling, and shimmery gold spirals hung down from them. In the center was a giant disco ball. Tess and Quinn had been working really hard today.

In one corner of the gym stood a three-dimensional tree with red apples hanging from its branches. And in another corner was a giant, glittery stack of hay, surrounded by real pumpkins and gourds.

But what made all of it so beautiful were the lights.

Streaks of gold light danced across the ceiling and walls and . . . dance floor.

Which was empty.

Whew.

Nick and Payton walked in together first, with Ox and me close behind. Groups of people stood around the perimeter of the room, talking or laughing or just standing there.

It was just a middle school dance. Why was I feeling so shaky?

"Emma! Payton!" Quinn emerged from one of the groups. "What do you think?" She waved her arms around the room.

"I think it looks wonderful," I said.

"And so do you," my sister added.

Quinn wore a blue dress with a gold belt and gold ballet shoes.

"You sparkle under the lights," I told her.

"Did you guys see the refreshments table?" Quinn pointed toward a crowded corner. "There's doughnuts and caramel apples and cookies and soda pop and apple cider."

"Oh yeah," Nick said. "I'm there."

"I'm coming with you," Ox said. "Uh, do you girls want anything?"

"A doughnut," Payton said.

"A cookie," I said.

"And cider," we both finished. "Please."

"I'm good," Quinn said, and we watched the boys walk quickly away. "Boys love their food! Good thing the parents donated a ton of refreshments."

We stood there, admiring one another's dresses and hair. Tess came over and joined us.

"Hey," she said.

"Hi!"

"You look great!" We gushed over her floral dress and her updo.

"Thanks," she said, smiling. "But I really meant 'hay,' as in, I've got hay down my back. Some guys were having a hay fight." She jumped up and down and, yep, pieces of hay fell out.

I admired the autumn leaves, some of which were peeling from the wall and fluttering to the ground. Like real autumn. I smiled.

"Ladies and gentlemen," a voice blasted through the room. "Welcome to the Autumn Dance, sponsored by the Parents Association and Student Council! I'm MC Adam, and I'll be your deejay tonight!"

Everyone cheered.

"The dancing is starting!" some girl yelled, and just then music started playing. Within seconds, a bunch of people were out in the middle of the floor, jumping and dancing around.

"It's all girls," Quinn laughed. She was right. The boys were either stuffing their faces with food or standing far away from the dance floor.

"Here you go." Ox and Nick came back with little plates and cups. I bit into a cookie and thought, *Mmm. Girls love their food too.*

"Oh no!" Quinn said. "The papier-mâché tree is leaning to one side. I've got to go save the tree!" She raced off.

"Is it all right if I hang out with you guys?" Tess asked shyly. "I mean, you have dates, so I don't want to be in the way."

"What?" Payton said. "Of course!" Soon a couple of Tess's friends came over, then a few of Nick's and some boys from the football team. Everyone was eating and talking.

And—I exhaled in relief—no one was dancing. Maybe . . . just maybe you didn't have to actually dance at a dance! A fast dance wrapped up.

"Let's give a special shout-out to our chaperones," MC Adam said.

Everyone clapped politely.

"One of our chaperones has a special request," MC Adam continued. "This song goes out to Counselor Case from Coach Babbitt."

Everyone went "Oooh! How romantic!" and made smoochy noises. Coach Babbitt took Counselor Case and led her to the dance floor.

I recognized the song immediately.

"Hey, that's the song from *Grease*!" I blurted out.

"Yes, it's Counselor Case's favorite movie," Jazmine James said behind me. "She even taught me the dance that goes with it. It's really hard, but I got it right away."

"Same here," I said.

Jazmine and I eyed each other. I might regret this, but I knew the one thing I could not do was back down from a challenge. Especially a challenge from Jazmine James.

"It's on," we both said at the same time, as if we were identical twins. Jazmine marched out onto the dance floor, her tangerine dress shimmering. She slipped off her silver heels. I followed suit.

And we both started to hand jive.

Pat, pat.

Clap, clap.

Goofy hand movements.

And thumbs-up over the shoulders.

People who were jumping around the dance floor turned to watch us. Soon, a spot was cleared out as they circled around us. Clap, clap! Pat, pat! Jazmine went faster! I went faster than Jazmine! She narrowed her eyes and went even faster! Jazmine and I were having a dance-off!

"Go, Emma!" I heard Payton yell.

"Go, Jazmine!" Hector countered.

Who was winning? It was hard to say! I was keeping up with Jazmine! She was keeping up with me. And then—

Counselor Case came over and joined us!

"Go, Louise!" Coach Babbitt yelled.

Clap, clap! Pat, pat! Counselor Case was hand jiving right along with me and Jazmine. Her eyes squinted at us, and she went faster. And faster . . . and holy moley, she was doing it so fast!

Jazmine and I glanced at each other. Then we tried to keep up but . . . there was no way. I clapped when I was supposed to pat. Jazmine patted when she was supposed to clap.

Counselor Case owned both of us.

The dance ended and we all stopped and stood there panting with exhaustion.

"Yeah! Counselor Case!" everyone was yelling.

"You won that dance-off." I held out my hand to Counselor Case. She shook it.

"I admit defeat." Jazmine shook Counselor Case's hand. "Most impressive."

Jazmine and I slunk off the dance floor. I glanced at her. She was glancing at me. Then we both started cracking up.

"We just got owned by Counselor Case," Jazmine said, shaking her head.

I was still cracking up when I returned to where my friends and sister were standing.

"You were great out there," Ox told me, handing me a cup of soda.

"Well, I faced my fear of dancing in public, I guess," I said. "At least the hand jive. Don't expect any other fast dancing."

"May I have your attention, Geckos! Hey! HEY!"

The music quieted down, and everyone turned to look at the stage where Sydney was yelling into the microphone.

"As you all know, I'm Sydney Fish!" Sydney's voice

filled the room. "Copresident of the dance committee!"

I started clapping. Payton raised an eyebrow at me and started clapping too. Hey, she had done a good job.

"I have an awesome surprise, arranged by me," Sydney said. "Thanks to me, we are going to have a special performance by the hottest new band in town. Fresh off their tour at Multipalooza, it's . . ."

This I had to see! I motioned my friends to move closer to the stage before everyone else did.

"THE SUPERTWINS!"

Sydney climbed down the steps and stood in front of us.

Asher, Dexter, and Oliver strode onto the stage. Asher and Oliver were carrying their guitars. They all looked psyched—even Asher. Their performance must have gone well today.

"We are the SuperTwins," either Dexter or Oliver said into the microphone. "And we want to play a song for our new school."

"And I want to introduce our newest member of the band." Asher leaned in. "Our lead singer, Cashmere."

"Wait, what?" Sydney blurted out.

Yup, Cashmere strode onto the stage. Cashmere, in a black rocker-chick T-shirt, ripped jeans, and black boots.

"What is she doing up there?" Sydney swiveled her head around to see if anyone knew.

"Singing, I guess." Payton shrugged.

That's right—Cashmere was a great singer, as we had learned on the double-decker bus in New York City.

"She's not only our new lead singer, she's also my date," Asher said shyly. Cashmere came over and gave him a hug.

"HEY!" Sydney yelled out. "He's my date! You can't steal my date!"

"Oh, stuff it, you can have the other two," Cashmere said into the microphone. "Here's a slow dance for all you people who can't fast dance."

Like me!

Nick took Payton's hand and led her to the dance floor.

"Emma, would you like to dance?" Ox asked.

I nodded. As I held out my hand, someone tugged on my dress.

"Emma! Emma! Dance with me?" It was Jason. Mason was right behind him.

"No, me!" Mason said.

"Sorry, guys, I'm already asked for," I said.

"I'd love to dance with you," Tess said. "May I?"

"I'm first!" Jason said, and dragged her out there.

❀ 211 ❀

"Hey, Mason, there's someone who needs a dance partner." I pointed toward the stage. Sydney was looking out sadly at the dance floor, since her two dates were playing.

"She's pretty," Mason said. He ran up to her, and I watched to make sure she was kind to him. She shrugged and went out to the dance floor. Sometimes, Sydney could be okay. Not often.

Ox took my hand and led me to the dance floor. We passed Jazmine and Hector slow dancing. Quinn and Ahmad from VOGS. Counselor Case and Coach Babbitt. Principal Patel and . . . Mrs. Burkle? We moved away from them.

I put my arms around Ox's neck. Our first slow dance! This was so romantic! This was so . . .

"Did you know that a hybrid of our names is a patented health care diagnostic device?" I blurted out.

Cashmere's voice sang softly as couples swayed around. Ox looked down at me.

"Oxemma," he said. "I know."

"You do?" I asked, moving my left foot, then my right foot in my best slow-dance move.

"Yeah," he said, and blushed. "I mashed our names on Wikipedia and found it."

I felt my face turn pink too.

We slow danced some more.

"Oof." Someone backed into me.

"Hey, Emma!" It was Mason. "Watch my smooth skills." He tried to twirl Sydney around. She had to duck under their hands awkwardly.

"Just don't dip me, shrimp," Sydney said, and they danced away.

"Cute hybrid," remarked Ox. "A shrimp and a fish. A crustaceanfish."

I got it. Because Sydney's last name was Fish. And I smiled. Because Ox got *me*. And he liked me anyway.

"You look really pretty," Ox said shyly.

"So do you," I said back shyly. "Handsome, I mean."

Ox bent down, his face coming closer to mine. Was he going to kiss me? He wasn't going to kiss me, was he? Not now! Not in front of all these people! I mean, it was all romantic and Ox was awesome, but I was only twelve, and I wasn't quite ready and . . .

"Emma," Ox said into my ear.

Oh! He was just going to say something to me.

"Did you know that an Emmox is a hybrid of intelligence and fun?" he said.

"Really?" I said. "I didn't know—"

Then I got it. Our own private mashup name.

"Oh . . . definitely," I said happily. "That's the coolest hybrid of all."

As the song ended, people started clapping around us. I stared into Ox's eyes.

"Dip me," I said in my most confident, competition-challenge voice.

And although I didn't know what I was doing, Ox gently leaned me back over his arm and dipped me.

And as he held me in his strong, muscley arms, I saw—upside down—Payton and Nick smiling at us and clapping. I smiled back and mouthed, "Squee!"

"Woot, Emma!" my twin said and punched the air.

I closed my eyes and smiled. Best. Romantic. Moment. Ever.

Payton

Twenty-five

MONDAY AFTER SCHOOL

We all huddled around the television monitor in the VOGS room.

"Good morning, Geckos!" Ahmad, the VOGS anchor, said on the television. "It's Tuesday, and we have a lot of news today."

It was actually still Monday, and it was after school. Mrs. Burkle had let us stay for a sneak preview of the VOGS cast that would be shown tomorrow morning at school.

"First," Ahmad reported, "it's Pasta Feasta day in the cafeteria, so come get your noodle on!"

I fidgeted in my chair.

"Are you so excited, Payton?" Tess asked. "Your first VOGS story on your own?"

"Excited, but also nervous and bracing myself," I said. "This has the potential to be very embarrassing."

I looked over at Emma. She was leaning on Ox's legs, peeking through her fingers.

"I can hardly look," Emma said.

"Nick, reassure us," I said.

"I promise you that the worst of it was edited out," Nick said. "Beyond that, no promises."

I smacked him lightly, and he grinned. We watched a segment about the new fire alarm system and then . . . There we were! Emma and me, in our colorful jackets!

"Squee!" I said. "And eek!"

Emma leaned forward. We both watched intently.

"We're live from Multipalooza!" On-screen Me said. "A festival for twins, triplets, and multiple identicals! I'm Payton! And this is *my* identical twin . . ."

"Emma!" Emma was on-screen now. "Have you ever wondered what's it like to have an identical twin or triplet? We'll be asking some of these thousands of people here."

The camera panned across the crowd. Suddenly, a now-familiar zombie face jumped up and started waving wildly at the camera.

"Tate!" Emma laughed. "I didn't know we were video-bombed by Tate!"

"And if you *haven't* wondered that," I was saying on camera, "perhaps you'll enjoy watching your fellow students humiliate themselves! Because I think that's going to happen today! Emma and I are challenging three of our newest Gecko classmates to an Identicals competition."

Emma and I both groaned.

"I can't look," I said. I buried my head in my arms and then peeked out.

"That's right—we have challenged Dexter, Oliver, and Asher, otherwise known as the SuperTwins, to a Multipalooza competition," Emma said.

And there we were!

First, at the Dizzy Plooza!

"Ohhhh!" Everyone in the room laughed and groaned and laughed. Mostly, I groaned. Embarrassing, painful— but excellent television.

Then there we were at the Multipaloo-Trivia. We all cheered as Emma hit buzzer after buzzer and won the game for us.

"We redeemed ourselves," Emma said.

Then the triplets zooming past us in the Three-Legged Race, as Emma and I fell flat on our faces.

"We unredeemed ourselves," I laughed.

Then the Tug-of-War! Nick got hilarious close-up shots of our ridiculous team—Mason and Jason with lizard face paint, the zombie kids, and us, trying so hard against the other team.

"That's painful!" Quinn said.

But then a shriek! And Mascot the Gecko had jumped on Dexter's head, and we all started howling with laughter! We were laughing so hard that Nick had to hit pause.

And then, the final Tug-of-War, where we all worked together on one team.

"Go, Geckos!" we all cheered at the end.

Then the scene shifted, and just Emma and I were on camera together. We had changed outfits.

"Ugh," I groaned. "This is when we have to do our wager because we lost. This is painful."

"I am wearing a T-shirt that says 'Triplets Are Three Times as Awesome,' Emma said, with a fake smile on her face.

"Mine says 'Triplets Rock!' Because Asher, Dexter, and Oliver really rock," I said. "SuperTwins rock."

"Triplets rule over Twins," Emma and I recited stiffly.

Suddenly a caption scrolled across the screen: *These statements are the result of a wager. They may or may not represent the views of VOGS anchors or staff.*

"Who did that?" Emma asked. I shrugged.

"Well, I figured it was journalistic integrity to be truthful," Nick said, and shrugged. "The viewers had a right to know."

We all laughed. I leaned over and gave Nick a hug.

The scene changed back to the middle of the festival. We saw faces of different people, people who looked alike and were dressing alike to celebrate being twins.

On-Screen Me began talking: "So let's find out what it's like to be an identical! There are over a thousand identicals here today, but I'll start by asking my own twin."

"That's a hard question to answer," Emma said. "I've never NOT been an identical, so I have nothing to compare it to."

"I thought you would answer it's the best thing in the world because you had *me* for a twin." I pretended to be disappointed.

"Sure, we'll go with that," Emma said with a grin.

"Let's ask our fellow Geckos: Asher, Dexter, and Oliver," I said. The camera panned over to the triplets. "What's it like being an identical?"

"Awesome," two of them answered. "You get a lot of attention."

❀ 219 ❀

"Although sometimes, you want to be an individual, so then it can be a pain," one said. Yep, that definitely would be Asher.

"Let's see what everyone else thinks!" On-Screen Emma said.

We went to interview people in the crowd.

"One of the coolest things about being a twin is that there's always someone who gets what you're talking about," a twin said.

"You have people that get you," said a certain zombie princess, with her zombie brother and sister.

"I love freaking people out when they don't know we're triplets," the triplet girls with the black curly hair said.

"You always have a best friend," another twin said.

The camera went back to me and Emma, standing together.

"That's all from our special on-the-scene VOGS cast," I said. "I'm Payton and this is—"

"I'm Emma," Emma said, interrupting me.

"You're supposed to just say Emma," I hissed at her.

"I didn't know," Emma said. "What do you think, I can read your mind or something? Twin telepathy?"

. . . and the screen went dark and everyone clapped. Emma and I most of all.

Emma

Twenty-six

AFTER SCHOOL

"What are Mom and Dad doing standing on our front porch?" I asked Payton. We'd just gotten off the bus and walked home from the bus stop.

"I have no idea," Payton said. She waved to them. They waved back.

"They're smiling," I observed. "So it's not bad news."

"Happy half birthday!" our parents called out.

I stopped. And did a quick calculation in my head. "We're twelve and a half today!" I said. With everything going on, we'd forgotten the Mills family tradition of celebrating the halfway point between birthdays.

Payton stopped too. "Only six months away from

being teenagers!" she exclaimed. We looked at each other.

Wow. Teenage twins . . . Twin teens . . .

"Emma! Payton!" Mom shouted. "Hurry!"

We hurried. All the way to our house and into our parents' arms. Because they grabbed us for hugs.

"Moom," Payton said. "You're smothering me. In public."

"I gave my father a squeeze and extricated myself from his grasp. I opened the front door and went inside, Payton right behind me. For a moment there was only the sound of our backpacks falling to the floor. Then . . .

"SQUEEEEEEEEE!!!"

My sister squealed the world's longest squee. I just stood there with my mouth open.

On the floor were two baskets. One had a pink bow, and the other had a blue bow. Peeking out from each basket—fluffy white fur and a pair of blue eyes.

Two baskets. Two . . .

"Kittens!" Payton and I shrieked.

"They're twins," Mom said. "Actually, twin girls."

"Twin kitties!" Payton sighed.

"Is the one with the blue bow for me?" I asked tentatively. I mean, we'd been pestering our parents about getting a pet for *years*. It seemed too good to be true.

"Happy half birthday!" Dad said. "And the one with the pink bow is for Payton. We got those colors right, didn't we?"

"Yes! Thank you!" Payton and I responded. We raced over to the baskets and sat down on the floor. Our parents continued on toward the kitchen, both smiling.

"Mew." My kitten—*my kitten!*—looked up at me and blinked. I put my face close to hers.

She gazed back at me. She looked intelligent.

"I'm going to name her Twinkle!" Payton said. I looked over and saw her kitten climbing out of its basket. "Her eyes are so twinkly! Emma, what are you going to name yours?"

"Einstein," I said.

"Einstein?" my sister said. "That's not a girl's name!"

I carefully picked up my kitten. She snuggled into my arms as I walked over to Payton.

"Okay," I said. "Princess Einstein. Called Einstein."

"Twinkle and Einstein." Payton sounded a bit doubtful. But then I put my kitten down near hers, and the two put their noses together.

"They're kissing!" said Payton. Then the kittens started playing with each other, rolling around on the floor.

And I admit it. I squeed.

Twenty-seven

TWO SECONDS LATER

Emma picked up her kitten and snuzzled it by her face.

"Um, are you sure about the name Einstein?" I asked.

"She likes Einstein," Emma said, turning to her kitten. "Don't you?"

"Mew," said her kitten.

"See? It's unanimous." My twin nodded firmly.

I scooped up Twinkle, who started purring like a little motor. "Presenting Twinkle and Einstein, the kitten twins," I said, holding Twinkle up.

"Or Einstein and Twinkle," Emma said. "Hey, do you think they're identical?"

We looked at each other's little fluffball and then back at our own.

"Well, mine's nose is a little more pink," said Emma. "And she's slightly larger than yours."

"Mine has a teensy bit bigger eyes," I observed. "And her tail is a little fluffier."

"The differences are infinitesimal," Emma said. "Therefore, I now pronounce you identical twin kittens!"

Just then, both kittens let out a big *"MEW!"*

I looked at Emma, and we both laughed.

"Twinx!" we said, our version of "jinx."

Twenty-eight

LATER THAT NIGHT

"Can you believe it's only been a few months since we started middle school?" Payton asked me.

"It sure has been eventful," I agreed.

We were home in our bedroom, Payton sitting on her bed with Twinkle, me lying down on mine with Einstein. It was nighttime, but neither of us could sleep. This was one of the times that made being a twin special. Just the two of us, talking about things no one else in the world would understand.

"I was trying so hard to fit in," Payton mused, dangling a piece of string so Twinkle could play with it. "And then . . . I oozed Ox."

"With a flying burrito," I remembered, laughing. Einstein was curled up against my neck, purring contentedly.

"And that," Payton said, "was the beginning of . . ."

"Twin Switches!" we both said at the same time.

"Twinx!" Then we sat in silence for a moment, just relaxing.

"Emma," my twin said. "Remember our first switch in the Janitor's Closet?"

"How could I forget?" I said.

"You're going to pretend to be me?" Payton had asked.

"Yes! I can be Payton with her head held up high," I had told her. *"Me, 'Payton' Mills. Well, for one afternoon anyway. That's just four periods."*

"Let's do it," Payton had said.

"And then we switched the next day on purpose," I remembered. "And you met Nick and told off Jazmine James in my math class."

"And you met Ox and showed off your new fashion skills to Sydney and Cashmere at the mall," Payton added.

"And I met Quinn," I said happily. "My first real friend." I scratched Einstein behind her ears, and she closed her eyes.

"But then the next day, things got all out of control with your crazy P equals E, E equals P chart," my twin said, while Twinkle pounced on the string and batted it around with her paws.

"You did meet Tess and get involved with VOGS," I reminded her. "So it wasn't a total disaster."

"You're right!" Payton smiled. "But then . . ."

"Jazmine James!" We both groaned. "Twinx!" Einstein opened one eye, then closed it again.

"Jazmine outing us on the live broadcast in front of the whole school was bad enough, but then we had to go fight with each other while the camera was still rolling," Payton continued.

"So embarrassing." I winced.

"Humiliating," Payton agreed.

"But then we redeemed ourselves by doing that truthful VOGS cast, and everything turned out okay," I said.

"Better than okay." Payton smiled.

I yawned, finally feeling a little sleepy. My twin and her kitten still seemed wide awake.

"But things got worse again," she said. "Our punishment for switching. Mine resulted in Sydney dumping a bucket of dirty water on my head."

"Right," I remembered. It led to our next Twin

Switch. "And just after that, I did *my* first community service and met . . ."

"Mason and Jason!" We both giggled. "Twinx!"

"And our friend, Mascot the Gecko." I rolled my eyes.

"Girls!" Our mom poked her head through the door. "It's late. Go to sleep."

"Good night," our dad said from the hallway.

"Good night, Mom! Good night, Dad!" I picked up Einstein and got out of bed. I carefully placed my kitten in her new bed. Payton carried her kitty over and put her down in the same bed. Payton and I stood there looking at the two little fluffballs, now both asleep.

"How adorable are they?" Payton said.

"Cutest kittens ever," I agreed. I turned off the light and climbed back in bed.

Our room was dark and quiet. Until I heard the *flump* of Payton flopping down in bed.

"Remember the Glinda bubble?" I whispered. This memory cracked Payton up.

"The *Wizard of Oz* play!" she snorted. "When I went under the stage to rescue Mascot . . ."

"And I had to go onstage in your place," I continued her sentence. "Performing as Glinda the Good Witch in her giant plastic bubble! Thank goodness you were able to switch back and finish the play. Which you were really good at. Hey, when we grow up, do you want to be an actor?"

"Maybe," Payton said. "I mean, I had such an amazing time in Hollywood acting in the shampoo commercial."

"Shiny, shiny, double the shiny," we both said, and then said, "TWINX!"

One of the kittens made a little "meow" sound.

"Shhh," I said.

We were quiet for a moment.

"And then we ran into Ashlynn from summer camp . . . ," Payton whispered.

"Summer *slave* camp for you," I whispered back. "But then Ashlynn got what she deserved, and you got to fall into Dustin Weaver's arms."

"More like fall *on* Dustin Weaver," Payton said. "But still, who'd have imagined I'd be that close to an actual celebrity? He was such a hottie."

"Cuter than Nick?" I teased.

"Ha-ha," my twin said. "Nick is totally cute and nice and fun and—when I went on that Ferris wheel in Times Square with him? That was . . . squee!"

"That whole trip to New York City was 'squee.'" I smiled.

"You said 'squee,'" Payton laughed quietly. "It sounds funny coming from a New York City math champion!"

"I did rock the Mathletes competition." I grinned. "First place! Oh yeah! I won!"

"That was awesome," Payton said. "But you know what my favorite part of our New York City trip was?"

"Embarrassing Sydney in front of a live, off-Broadway audience?" I guessed.

"No, although she totally deserved it," Payton said. "It was when you and I were sitting together on top of the double-decker bus touring New York City. The sights and sounds and city breeze through our hair . . ."

"The tree branch in your face," I giggled.

"Okay, maybe not that," my twin said.

"Just kidding," I said. "That was an amazing time, wasn't it?"

"Definitely," Payton said. Then she yawned. Which made me yawn. Which made her yawn again.

"Payton?" I said. "Wasn't Multipalooza amazing too? Even though we accidentally switched places and lost to those triplets?"

"It was," Payton agreed. "And we all came together at the end and supported Mason and Jason."

"No matter how different we all are from each other," I said, "in the end, we're all Geckos."

"That sounded really deep," Payton said. "And really weird."

"You know what I mean," I told her. "We're all on the same team."

"But not as close as Team Mills," my twin said.

"That's right," I said. "Twins rule!"

"Emma?" Payton said. "Wasn't our first dance special?"

"Exceptional," I said. I wanted to talk about it more, in detail, but I was getting really sleepy. We could relive it together, tomorrow.

"You know," Payton said, "switching places caused us a bunch of trouble, but it also changed our lives forever. If we hadn't switched, I wouldn't have gotten drama or VOGS cast . . . or gotten to know Nick and Tess."

"And I realized that academics and winning wasn't everything, made my first real friend, and, well, then there's Ox."

"Squee," Payton whispered.

"Woo-hoo!" I said quietly, and punched the air in the dark.

"Did you just do one of your punches?" Payton asked. "I could hear the awkwardness in the air."

"What?" I said. "I don't hear anything. Or anyone. La la la, I'm all alone. This is what it must be like to be an only child."

"Emma?" my sister said in a small voice. "Would you rather be an only child?"

"Are you kidding me? No!" I said. "You're my best friend! Nobody gets me like you do!"

"Thanks," Payton said. "Ditto."

"Besides, who else could I trade places with?" I joked.

"Seriously," said Payton. "Do you think we'll ever switch places again?"

"I'd like to say no . . ." I said slowly.

"But never say never," Payton finished.

"Just twins forever," I added, smiling.

"Twinky swear?" said Payton. "I'm holding up my pinkie finger."

I held mine out too, and imagined we were linking pinkies. "Ready," I said.

"Twins forever," we both said. "Twinky swear."

I put my hand down and smiled. In the dark I could tell that Payton was smiling too.

And before either of us could say "Twinx!" we were asleep in our twin beds.

Acknowledgments

Triple thanks to:

The family: Dave DeVillers, Greg Roy, Quinn DeVillers, Jack DeVillers, Adam Roy, and Robin Rozines.

The Simon & Schuster crew: Fiona Simpson, Bethany Buck, Mara Anastas, Alyson Heller, Annie Berger, Paul Crichton, Lucille Rettino, Carolyn Swerdloff, Karin Paprocki, Katherine Devendorf, and Martha Hanson.

Mark McVeigh.

The Saratoga Springs supporters: Melinda, Claudia and the SIS girls; the Ginley and Greenfield girls; Margaret and Lake Avenue Elementary and Emily Mattison.

Triple thanks to Paige Pooler! Paige Pooler! Paige Pooler!

And to all our Payton and Emma readers!